Sickled Shock

Thunderous Blood: The Hero with Sickle Cell

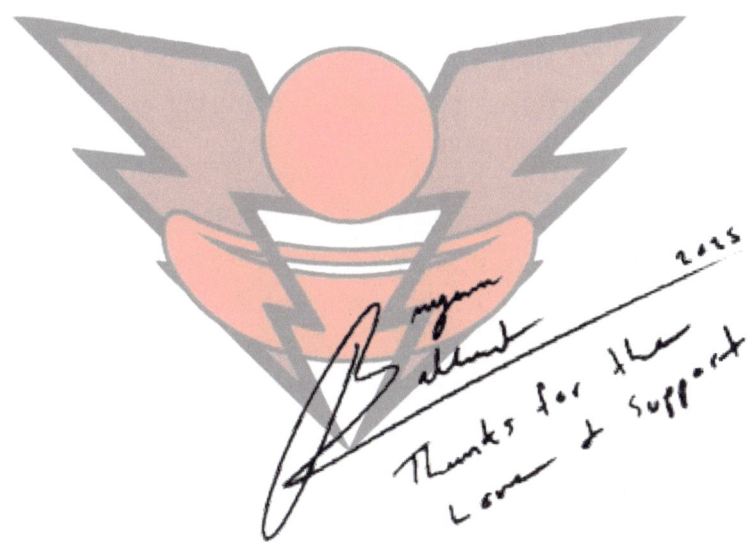

Bryan Ballard

Sickled Life Inc.
Sickled Shock,
Thunderous Blood: The Hero with Sickle Cell

ISBN: 979-8-218-61384-6
First Edition: April 2025
Cover design by: Bryan Ballard
Book written by: Bryan Ballard

Printed in the USA.
sickledlife.com

Living the Sickled Life comes with tremendous battles of ups and downs. One cannot get discouraged and let Sickle Cell determine the future!

For I know the plans I have for you," declares the LORD, "plans to prosper you and not to harm you, plans to give you hope and a future.

-Jeremiah 29:1

Table of Contents

Preface 9

Thunderous Blood: The Hero with Sickle Cell............... 11

1 A Cry of Strength 13

2 Strange Results 21

3 A Night of Decisions.................................... 29

4 Questions in the Dark.................................. 35

5 The Mystery of Sickle Cell............................. 42

6 Chasing Shadows 53

7 Beyond the Pain....................................... 63

8 Buried Secrets 68

9 The Calm Before the Storm 74

10 The Calm Before the Hunt............................ 81

11 Starting Strong 87

12 The Science of Us.................................... 93

13 Behind Closed Doors.................................102

14 Shadows of the Storm 111

15 Lightning in the Veins...............................122

16 The Weight of the Past 128

17 In the Wake of Shock 134

18 Hidden Truths 140

19 Dr. Vial...146

20 Thunderous Blood 152

21 Tensions Rise 160

22 Sickled Shock 168

23 The Ultimate Plan 178

24 Full Circle 185

Quote from Sickle Cell 195

Other titles by author 197

WARNING

The content of this book is purely fictional. The science experiments, stunts, and health-related scenarios, including any mention of medications, treatments, or physical activities, should NOT be attempted in real life.

The author and publisher do not endorse, recommend, or condone any actions, experiments, or health practices described in this work. The science presented, while based on creative imagination, may involve unsafe or unrealistic practices.

Health and Safety Disclaimer:
Any mention of health, medication, or medical treatments in this book is fictional and should not be used as a substitute for professional medical advice. Always consult with a qualified healthcare provider before making any decisions regarding your health, medications, or treatments.

FACTUAL INFORMATION ABOUT SICKLE CELL

While this book contains fictional elements, it does include factual information about sickle cell disease. Sickle cell is a real, genetic blood disorder affecting millions worldwide. It is characterized by abnormal hemoglobin, which causes red blood cells to form a crescent or "sickle" shape, leading to various health complications. This information is based on established medical knowledge. For accurate details or concerns, please consult a healthcare professional or trusted medical resource.

Preface

Every day, millions live with the unspoken reality of chronic illness—sickle cell disease. For those battling it, life requires unyielding courage, strength, and resilience. But what if these warriors were more than survivors? What if they were superheroes?

This book is my tribute to the true heroes: the Sickle Cell Warriors. Born from my own experience, it's a reminder that we are not defined by our condition. We are fighters, and now, we are superheroes.

The protagonist embodies the strength I see in every warrior—rising above the pain, harnessing the power of lightning to inspire and protect. This isn't just fiction; it's a celebration of resilience, hope, and the unbreakable spirit of the sickle cell community.

To every warrior who faces the daily struggles of sickle cell disease, this story is for you. You are powerful, unstoppable, and worthy of the same admiration as any superhero.

With this book, I hope to raise awareness, shed light on the realities of living with sickle cell, and offer a symbol of strength and pride to all who fight this battle. You are not alone.
This is our story. This is our time.

The Sickle Cell Warriors now have their superhero.

Thunderous Blood: The Hero with Sickle Cell

Chapter 1

A Cry of Strength

I t all started on a gloomy Monday night in Portsville, with rain and thunderstorms filling the air. It wasn't the greatest Monday for most, but for the Lorane family, it was a day of beauty and joy. On January 24th, 2095, their baby boy, Cain, was born. It was a day of overwhelming emotions—such a rollercoaster—but ultimately a blessing, as Cain's birth was a success. However, that joy quickly turned to fear when the doctor entered the room and informed them that Cain had been diagnosed with sickle cell anemia.

"What does that mean for our baby boy, Doc?"

the parents asked.

"*With the recent advances in research, there are now medicines available that can help reduce crises. It's also possible to perform a bone marrow transplant without a sibling donor, although having a sibling is typically linked to a higher success rate. However, we only recommend the transplant if the disease becomes severe.*"

– Of course, the year 2095 and still no perfect cure for sickle cell. –

Boom! Crack! Thunder rumbled, and a flash of lightning lit up the sky outside the hospital window. When would things get better for the sickle cell community?

As rain streaked down the hospital window and the sound of a baby's cry filled the room, the Lorane family now faced the challenge of raising a warrior. With everything going on, doctors now take baby Cain for more test. While the nurses had baby Cain and the mother could take a mental break on everything she pulls out her phone to write a quick poem that came to her mind:

01/24/2095

WHY MY CHILD

I KNEW IT WAS IN THE FAMILY
NEVER THOUGHT IT WOULD HAPPEN TO ME

```
         I NEVER ASKED MY HUSBAND
           WE NEVER TOOK THE TEST
        WE NEVER KNEW WE WOULD GIVE HIM
            THE SICKLE CELL DISEASE
     MY HUSBAND AND I DECIDED TO HAVE A CHILD
  NEITHER OF US KNEW WE HAD SICKLE CELL TRAIT
      I ALWAYS WANTED A LITTLE BOY TO SPOIL
         GOD GAVE US A VERY SPECIAL ONE
        ONE WHO WILL GET A LOT OF ATTENTION,
          MEDICATION AND DOCTOR VISITS
                 A LOT OF LOVE
            GOD NOT ONLY GAVE US CAIN,
      BUT GAVE CAIN US HIS CARE TAKERS HIS
             GAURDIANS, HIS PARENTS
         EVERY DAY WE TELL HIM WE LOVE HIM
       GOD KNEW THIS ONE WOULD BE TAKEN CARE OF

              THATS WHY MY CHILD
```

As she finishes with her poem, the nurses are now with baby Cain in the pediatric part of the hospital to continue tests to ensure a healthy growth and looking out for any other issues. During the test, the thunder and lightning caused a surge that triggered the hospital's power to flicker, followed by a spark that sent the lights out. Luckily, the backup generators kicked in immediately, restoring power to the hospital. During all that an electrical shock went throughout baby Cains body from being hooked up to all the machines and sending him into a screaming cry. None of the doctors or nurses noticed the electrical surge affecting the baby. They assumed his crying was simply due to the thunder.

After all the tests came back successful the nurse then returned baby Cain to his parents nice and wrapped up, no more crying and doing perfectly fine. This electrical shock could cause problems later in life, but Cain had already proven how strong he was—both as a baby and as the sickle cell warrior he would grow to be. As well as lifelong problems this static charge could have easily killed baby Cain before his life started. However, he took the shock with just a loud screaming cry. Who would have thought 30 minutes into life a baby could go through so much and still have a lot more to fight through while dealing with sickle cell in life.

About an hour or so goes by and the Lorane family is finally settled down and resting in the hospital room. On the other side it's a nurse who isn't quite as settled down as the family. In fact, she's in pure panic and confusion over an hour after the power went out.

From down the hall another nurse yells out "Nurse Van!?"

She turns and looks at the nurse who is motioning her over. As Van approaches the other nurse she gets questioned.

"Hey Van, are you okay? You haven't really been the same since the power went out." Says nurse

Elaine.

"Yeah, Ye ye ye yeah, I'm fine." As Van answers nervously.

She then proceeds to look up at Elaine knowing she wasn't fine. She then proceeds to grab Elaine by the arm and pulls her into the nursing station.

"Van what are you..."

"Shhh! Listen... you know that baby in room 420?" As she interrupted Elaine.

"Yea he is so cute, isn't he? I hate that he must grow up fighting sickle cell."

"No, no listen..." Nurse Van then begins to whisper, "He should be dead." In a frantic face.

"WHAT!" yells nurse Elaine.

"Shhh" Van shushes her again. "Listen; when the power went out, he was hooked up to the machines and I watched him get electrocuted to the point that it could've killed any of us adults. All that happened though was his eyes jolted open and back closed, then he burst out in a screaming cry."

"That's impossible Van, you might be losing it."

"Listen Elaine, have you ever seen a newborn baby with bright yellow eyes?"

"I mean he does have sickle cell Van; you do remember jaundice is a thing and can cause a yellow tint within the eyes."

"No Elaine, you're not understanding me. Yes of course, I know what jaundice is. His EYES Elaine,

HIS EYES were glowing yellow. Like a bright lightning yellow from the sky."

"Okay I'll tell you what Van. I'm going to take this chart in to fill out and ill check his eye color for the documents and we will go from there."

"Okay fine but I'm telling you, that baby is different."

Soft knocks come from outside of Lorane's family room, as the door opens.

"Hello, I'm nurse Elaine taking over for Van for a little. I'm here to get baby Cains height, weight, hair and eye color. Quick and easy and I'll let y'all rest"

Elaine carefully approaches baby Cain with a soft "aww he's so cute, congratulations."

She stretches Cain out to measure a long 20 inches and then proceeds to place him on the scale for a weight of 8 pounds and 10 ounces.

"Wow mom you have a big boy on your hands." Says the nurse.

"Yeah, hopefully a football player" says the dad.

"Now I will chart his hair and eye color and be on my way."

The nerves start to hit her now as she starts thinking about everything nurse Van had told her just a few minutes ago.

As a slight bead of sweat runs down her back,

she goes to lift the baby's eyelid to the surprise of baby Cain and his light brown eyes. She then charts that plus his black hair. Nurse Elaine then returns baby Cain to the mom and exits the room.

Elaine goes back to the nursing office to no surprise a nervous, scared nurse Van.

"So good news" Elaine says. "Baby Cain is nice and healthy and should be able to go home tomorrow morning."

"Umm Elaine, aren't you leaving out some details." asked Van with a worried look on her face.

"No, what details?"

Nurse Van jumps out of her seat and says "His eyes! What about his eyes Elaine?"

"Oh" Gasped Elaine. "They are so cute and adorable right?"

"ELAINE enough!"

"You know I'm a nervous wreck after what I saw."

"Relax Van he is fine. His eyes are a soft light brown, almost like beach sand."

"So, no yellow?" asked Van.

"No, No yellow at all."

Nurse Van sits back in her chair with a worried look on her face while shaking her head.

"I'm telling you now Elaine baby Cain is different and I'm not sure how he is alive."

"Well Van he is, and he is healthy. It's not much we can do now so get back to your shift. Maybe go wash your face with cold water or something to refresh yourself."

"Okay yeah, you're right Elaine, go wash my face and continue my night shift like I didn't just witness a baby get electrocuted and open his eyes with static yellow eyes in between the power shifting to the generator. Let's do that!"

Van aggressively gets up and storms out as other nurses walk in the break room. What's wrong with her, they ask Elaine.

"Nothing, she's just having a bad day. She should be fine."

Van does as Elaine suggests and washes her face and continues her night. Before her shift is over, she apologizes to Elaine.

"You're right Elaine, and I'm sorry for blowing up on you. I still stand on the fact that he will be a different type of baby though. Don't be surprised when this all comes full circle."

Chapter 2

Strange Results

As night turned to early morning, the Lorane family prepared to go home. The night shift nurses have now gone home and been replaced by the morning shift. Back at home nurse Van still isn't feeling comfortable about the situation that occurred with baby Cain. In fact, she begins her own little research and types up a quick summary of what she had witnessed that night.

Before sitting down on the couch, Van quickly prepared a simple dinner—rice and spicy sausage for jambalaya. Once the meal was nearly done, she set the pot on the back burner, lowering the heat to a simmer. She then pulled out her laptop and sat on the couch, beginning her research.

Van goes on to look up many different topics just to get a general idea of things. Including how many volts can a human intake before harm, babies getting shocked, how much current runs through specific hospital equipment, yellow eyes, static electricity within the eyes. Her research goes on and on, all while typing up things she experienced just hours ago. Her paper was rough and rushed, as exhaustion from her shift and the situation with baby Cain weighed on her. It read as follows:

I, Van, am a nurse with 15 years of experience. I'm writing this not only to get everything off my chest but also to document these events for myself, in case I need to reflect on them later. I'm nervous to inform anybody else as I don't know if this will be a problem for me and my job later in the future. What I experienced just hours ago on my January 24th, 2095, shift was something I have never seen in all 15 years plus of my nursing career.

Within these specific long 2 hours of my shift, I was in charge of getting medical information and tests for a newborn baby along with other team members. During this test the power ended up tripping off due to the weather we were having here in Portsville. As my medical staff scrambled and looked around to try to restore power and see what happened. I was dead focused on the baby during the test for his health. Mind you when the power shut down it was a brief 2-3 seconds, but for me it seemed like 2-3 minutes.

During this brief moment, I witnessed the baby get shocked in a way that seemed impossible. His eyes opened wide, glowing yellow with what appeared to be a static charge pulsing within his pupils. When the power flickered back on, his eyes snapped shut, and he let out a piercing scream. My coworkers thought he was afraid of the loud thunder; little do they know I'm pretty sure he is crying in pain. A coworker yells at me from a distance not realizing what I just saw and tells me to unplug everything and swaddle the baby to calm him down. I do as I was told, but in such disbelief on how this baby even has a cry in him or even still alive. I recently got home and typed this up as well as some research on the situation.

With a little research, I found that 150mA can be fatal, while 10mA can cause severe muscle contractions. I suspect he could have easily died from just 5mA, given that he's a newborn and hooked up to direct current. I'm saying all this to say; that baby is different, and I wouldn't expect anything less than this coming back up in the near future and being a problem. I'm signing out with that.

- Nurse Van

She saves the document, closes her laptop and was instantly reminded of the cooking she was doing with the smell of burnt rice. She jumps up and saves whatever is not burnt and continues her late morning with sleep for the day.

Back at the hospital, the Lorane family packed up their belongings, preparing to take baby Cain home to the comfort of his own home. Despite the shock, baby Cain had been behaving like any typical newborn. Let's not forget that he has sickle cell and has more in life to fight through, not just that electrical shock. With that his crying could mean many different things from the normal newborn cries to the pain of sickle cell anemia. Before fully being released the doctor orders blood work to check out the baby's hemoglobin and blood levels to insure a healthy discharge from the hospital.

Moments later the nurse comes in to take Cains blood. While drawing his blood it all looks normal and comes out easily and red just as it should. Things end up getting interesting later though. The nurse goes on as normal and takes the tubes of blood to the lab for them to test his hemoglobin. The lab used only half of the vials, placing the remainder in the blood bank for future disposal. Thirty or so minutes go by, and the doctors come back to Lorane's family room with news that would be unexpected.

"Hello, I'm the doctor for the evening, and all the blood work has come back. Now as we know your baby boy has been diagnosed with sickle cell anemia. However, the blood levels have come back with some interesting results. It's still showing signs of sickle cell, buts its his hemoglobin that has us all confused. This confusion causes concern, but it's a good case of concern in a way. When baby Cain was first born his hemoglobin level was at a 5.9 which would be a concern for someone without sickle cell. The result now shows that his hemoglobin is a 12.8 which is shocking results for anyone who is a sickle cell patient. In fact, this may be the record high for highest hemoglobin for any sickle cell patient I have seen personally. The

lowest hemoglobin I've ever seen was in another sickle cell patient—his was as low as 2.7. I still don't know how he managed to walk into the hospital. Now with baby Cains hemoglobin being so high over a 24-hour period we may need to do follow-up appointments more often. Instead of every two to three months lets shoot for once a month as well as back here in two weeks for a follow up."

The Lorane family agreed and has now officially been discharged. With that the Lorane family is finally able to be on the way to the comfort of their own home.

As the Lorane family stepped out of the hospital, something unexpected happened: the power went out, from the front doors all the way through to the back of the building. It instantly came back on, but of course everyone is still thinking it's a power surge because of the storm from last night. All I can say is good thing nurse Van didn't see this. She would've really flipped out. She did say it would all end up coming full circle.

When the power returned, Dr. Sam Bloodworth went to the blood bank to check the temperature and ensure it had returned to the proper level. This is where things get interesting. When Sam Bloodworth goes in he notices a vial of blood had a certain glow to it. He assumed it was a reflection of light coming off the vial. When he gets closer to fully inspect the vial, he realizes the blood is glowing with a yellow tent to it. He was now deeply confused and, in a panic, ran the numbers on the vial through the system. The numbers, however, do not pull up any patients within the system.

The air in the room becomes hot as Sam is now panicking even more now that the numbers on the vial don't connect to any patients. Without thinking he quickly calls over to a coworker of his who is in the lab next to him, when he arrives in the blood bank fridge with Bloodworth, he is instantly confused when he also sees the glowing vial of blood.

"Ummm...is that normal?"

"What do you think? NO, not at all! Plus, I looked up the vial number in the system and it's coming up with an error saying no patient information in the system matching that number."

"Why doesn't it have the patients name on it?"

"Once the lab physician uses the needed amount of blood, they send the extra over to us for a later disposal. Once it arrives here the patients' names are stripped off the vial for security reasons and then we hold until further notice of disposal."

This now leaves both physicians in disbelief. How can this blood be glowing yellow like it is and who did it come from? They now must figure out what to do and how many others to tell. This seems like a serious situation that could end badly. So, their next move needs to be smart cause it could also cost them their job for tampering with patient records. Sounds like nurse Van was right, baby Cain is different and going to be a problem.

Chapter 3

A Night of Decisions

The next day, unironically the hospital held its scheduled nurses' meeting. These meetings typically cover patient care, hospital issues, and sometimes feature special guests discussing specific diseases. Normally held at the start of the 7 p.m. shift, tonight's meeting had been pushed to the end of the shift due to the high number of patients and tasks. Nurse Van was excited to hear that the meeting was pushed back, giving her time to consider bringing up the situation she encountered or not.

During Van's shift, she bumped into nurse Elaine.

"Hey, Elaine, can I talk to you for a second?"

"Sure, what's going on?" Elaine responded.

Nurse Van gave Elaine a look that said, *you know what I'm talking about.*

Then proceeds to ask her *"What should I do tonight? Should I bring up the baby situation?"*

"I'll be honest, Van. If you bring that up, I don't think anyone will believe you. I barely believe it myself. But I'm here to support you, and I want to help ease your mind. In the end, it's up to you."

"Yeah, you're right. They probably won't believe me. I'll just let it play out and see how things go during the meeting. Besides, with tonight's topic being sickle cell and patient management, it might be the perfect time to bring it up. Thanks, Elaine."

The two nurses go back to their shift until the meeting later that night. In the small city of Portsville, the hospital was far from large. Small city, small hospital—word traveled quickly, especially in the more secluded parts of the facility, like the Blood Bank.

Let's just say that things didn't stay quiet in the Blood Bank the way they did in the nursing station. The glowing vial was now the talk of the Blood Bank, and no one knew what to make of it or how to handle the situation. Now the whole night shift is involved with it. Guess it's easier to keep a secret of what you saw versus what can be physically seen. This vial of blood is still glowing, but not as bright as it was around 10 hours ago.

With Dr. Sam Bloodworth being the head physician in charge of the Blood Bank called upper management to cover himself and his job. He asked if it was permissible to take samples from a vial discharged by doctors, with no patient names attached. The overhead physician informs him that it is not safe nor legal to do so, and she strongly advises against it. He acknowledges what she said and hangs up the phone.

Did Sam listen to whoever was on the other side of the phone? Of course not. Sam Bloodworth ends up taking samples and notices an abundance of sickled shaped red blood cells. An unnormal number of sickled cells at that. Especially compared to the amount of normal red blood cells he sees.

Sam muttered under his breath, "Oh wow, this patient has sickle cell, and an abnormal number of sickled red blood cells in this test. He or she must still be hospitalized."

He quickly cleaned up any evidence and returned the vial to the Blood Bank as if nothing had happened. On his way out of the blood bank he runs into a nurse in the hall.

"Hey, do you know what today's meeting is about, or if any special guests are joining?" he asked the nurse.

She responds with "I think it's about sickle cell, patient management, and that there could be a sickle cell specialist of sorts joining."

"Oh really?" he responded with a shocking look on his face.

He attempts to just walk away thanking her, but the nurse was too curious as to why he asked that.

"Excuse me, what made you ask, if you don't mind me asking?"

"Oh no reason, sometimes I like joining in to learn new things."

She thinks nothing of it and says, "Oh okay, you just seemed really shocked when I said sickle cell."

"No, I just don't know too much about sickle cell, so I was excited to join and learn more about it tonight."

The conversation doesn't last much longer after that, and they both go about their day.

The time for the meeting was fast approaching, and Van had been watching the clock like a hawk. She is still trying to figure out if she should bring up the situation on what happened with baby Cain or not. She wasn't the only one anxiously watching the clock; Sam Bloodworth was also waiting for the meeting with a sense of urgency. One of the early morning nurses ended up arriving early relieving nurse Van from her shift earlier than normal. Nurse Van ran her rounds with the nurse quickly showing her all her patients for the morning and what's been going on. After she is finished, nurse Van ends up at the meeting room 5 minutes early. Here she can finally relax and think solely about what she will do for the meeting.

Surprisingly enough the next person to show up early for the meeting was Sam Bloodworth. While neither realizes they are both worried about the same situation they do nothing but acknowledge each other.

"Hey, nurse Van, right?" Sam Bloodworth says.

"Yeah, that's me. You're Dr. Sam Bloodworth from the blood bank, right? hey how are you doing?"

"Yes, but please just call me Bloodworth. I'm pretty good and yourself?"

"I'm not complaining."

And that was the end of the conversation. Quick and out the way as they are both worried about other things and not the conversation at hand.

Soon after 7:05 am the meeting room is pretty filled up at this point and the meeting soon to start. Elaine ended up being the second to last person to arrive at the meeting.

Instantly as Elaine walks through the doors she is met by a voice. "Oh, Elaine, I'm so glad to see you! I was afraid you wouldn't make it to the meeting," Van said.

"Yeah, I'm here, one of my patients needed some extra assistance at the last minute so I'm a little late. What have I missed so far?" she asked all while taking a seat next to Van.

Van started to answer, "Nothing, it hasn't sta—" but was interrupted when the head doctor walked in with several others. Conversations in the room stopped instantly, and everyone's attention turned to the front.

Chapter 4

Questions in the Dark

The head doctor began introducing the guests she had brought with her—another doctor, three nurses, and a top medical student nearing graduation from PVU. He had just completed his master's in microbiology and was on track to earn his Ph.D., with a focus on sickle cell awareness.

The doctor introduces him as "Clark Watson". Clark introduced himself to the nursing staff who had been waiting. As he told the staff they will learn a little more about sickle cell anemia and the procedures to take if a patient was to come in dealing with complications from sickle cell. Before Clark began, he mentioned that he hoped to become a school science teacher, so this meeting would be a good place to start. He hoped to teach the nurses something new or, at the very least, refresh their knowledge of sickle cell anemia and patient care.

Clark Watson goes on and starts his lesson by telling the nursing staff to feel free to just call him Clark as he hasn't personally claimed any of his titles just yet and continues on with the lesson.

"If you have any questions during this meeting feel free to ask and I will also ask if any questions are needed after I finish. I will try to make this quick as I know you all just got off and it's late-night early morning.

"Safe to assume that everyone here is familiar with sickle cell, a blood disorder where cells take on a banana shape, causing blockages in the blood vessels and leading to various complications within the body. These problems can include strokes, acute chest syndrome, organ damage, ulcers, and many other problems, and the most common problem is a sickle cell pain crisis.

A pain crisis happens when these sickle-shaped cells get stuck in the blood vessels, causing a blockage. This blockage leads to intense pain in whatever part of the body is affected.

Sickle cell is not contagious. In fact, it's a hereditary condition passed down through generations. Sickle cell also comes in many different variations including the sickle cell trait and sickle cell disease without going into details. The chance of a child receiving the full-blown disease is 25% if both parents have the trait.

Now as for patient care and management for sickle cell patients. The care for a patient will be very different for each patient, but at the same time it should be similar at the start. First and foremost, we must acknowledge every patient's pain as REAL and avoid judging them based on how they express it during a sickle cell pain crisis. All crises are different, all patients are different, and pain tolerance is different within every patient. As the nurse or doctor we should always listen to our patients as they would know way more about what helps them verse what does not help. They live with this disease, we do not. That is the motto we should apply to dealing with a sickle cell patient. I will say that again... **They live with this disease, we do not.** Sickle cell patients are not drug seekers, and we should never classify them as such.

I suggest the proper procedure for a patient with sickle cell pain should start with an immediate IV and start a saline drip. We should also offer the patient oxygen as it isn't always needed but it helps for some even if their O2 levels are good. Once we have successfully accomplished a IV line, a saline drip, and offered oxygen to the patient we can now wait on doctor's orders but should be pushing a quick dose of pain medicine to make the patient comfortable. From here we then figure out our next steps to getting proper pain *management going and learning about the patients' care. Including having an open ear and listening to patient's parents or loved ones as they would know a lot more than we do when it comes to the care of the patient. Pain management and patient care for sickle cell anemia should never be based on previous cases. I can't stress this enough—every sickle cell patient is different, and their pain management should reflect that.*

As I was saying earlier, I don't want to keep you all long, so I will end with that and ask if you have any questions regarding sickle cell and/or patient care within?"

One of the nurses raises her hand, and ask the question *"What's an average hemoglobin for sickle cell patients, and do their blood cells last as long as normal red blood cells?"*

During this question Bloodworth as well as nurse Van are still looking for a good time within the meeting to drop their questions.

"Well, a hemoglobin of a sickle cell patient can vary anywhere between 6 and 11. Compared to a person without sickle cell of around a 12 hemoglobin. As for your second question, their blood cells do not last as long as someone without sickle cell. In fact, a sickle cell patient's red blood cells last 10 to 20 days compared to someone without sickle cell red blood cells lasting 120 days."

Elaine leans over and whispers to Van *"What did you decide about your question?"*

"I'm not sure yet."

During the conversation between Elaine and Van Bloodworth raises his hand.

"Yes sir" says Clark.

"Uhm yes, I've heard of jaundice within a patient, usually within their eyes. I was just wondering if it could cause the blood of a sickle cell patient to be a different color or have any yellow tent to the blood at all?"

Van and Elaine exchanged puzzled glances, both unsure of what was happening.

"No not usually blood in a sickle cell patient should be as normal as any other patient with a red or possibly a darker red if dehydrated."

In a sudden panic, Van sprang to her feet, raising her hand while blurting out her questions:

"Can sickle cell cause any unusual resistance to things like pain or even static shock? Also, can babies' eyes show a yellow bolt of light or glow, and is there any difference in hemoglobin in newborns?"

Elaine, along with the rest of the room, stared at Van in confusion as the silence hung thick. The room remains quiet as Van looks around and slowly sits back down. Clark eventually responds to Van in a nervous voice as he is confused about what is going on.

"Well, I'll do my best to answer everything. Yes, sickle cell can cause a yellow tint in the eyes, but there's no resistance to static or anything else. Hemoglobin in babies is no different either. I hope that answers your questions, though I must admit, I'm a bit confused by some of them."

The room remains silent even after Clark gives an answer to Van. Bloodworth, intrigued, couldn't help but wonder what had driven Van to ask such frantic, personal questions. *Those questions sounded deeply personal,* he thought.

Clark once again breaks the silence in the room saying *"Well if there are no more questions that will end my part of the meeting. I hope we can do this again soon as I love the knowledge and study of sickle cell. Have a good night."*

The head doctor goes over a few more little details and then dismisses the meeting from there. Everyone starts to walk out leaving Van with her head down on the table in embarrassment. Elaine asks if she was okay.

Van responds and tells her *"Yes I'm fine, now leave me alone."*

Elaine joins the rest of the group as they all slowly walk out of the meeting room. Suddenly a hand rest on Vans shoulder.

Van reacts by saying "*I told you I'm fine, now leave me alone.* She notices that Elaine didn't listen and instead sat down next to her.

"*Look I told you to leave me alone*"

As Van raises her head to look at Elaine, she quickly realizes it isn't Elaine. In fact, it's Bloodworth from the blood bank. She quickly responds with an apology.

"*Oh, hey I'm sorry. I thought you were someone else checking on me. I didn't realize it was you I am so sorry.*"

It's a slight and awkward 3 second pause before Bloodworth responds...

Bloodworth, his face filled with concern and curiosity, leaned in and said, "*I think we need to talk.*"

Chapter 5

The Mystery of Sickle Cell

At home now, the Lorane family is just preparing for worst case scenario. Raising a child is hard, but now they must learn how to raise a baby with sickle cell anemia. This could be a tough task, but if Van is right about baby Cain maybe this won't be such a hard task for the family as expected. Growing up with sickle cell is just as hard as raising a baby with sickle cell. The Lorane family is in for a ride either way now that they have brought a blessing of life into their home.

The family begins with general research on the topic of sickle cell. Doing so all while raising a newborn for the first time. Shockingly enough, baby Cain has been doing pretty well since he's been home and released from the hospital. This doesn't stop the family from doing their research. During their research they have learned small details and interesting facts about it all. Including things that may be shocking to them and not the best to read over the internet.

Through the research they decided they wanted to know how they both received the trait and if anyone else had it within their family. Momma Lorane started off with a phone call to her parents. She asks them if they knew anything about sickle cell and if anyone had it. Shockingly enough both of her parents knew about sickle cell but never realized it could become a problem. Momma Lorane asked her father why they never talked about it. He goes on to answer with.

"Well baby girl I grew up with the trait and never had any problems dealing with sickle cell. Your mother never had anyone in her family with it and I've never personally known anyone with it. Apparently, my grandfather had the disease, but I didn't know him, and I definitely didn't expect it to come full circle affecting my grandson. With all this brand-new technology and advanced health,

I'm sure he will be fine and live life amazingly if that's what you're worried about baby girl."

"Yeah, dad you're right I was just curious on our family history with sickle cell that's all. I love you and see you next week."

The phone call ends.

Now as for Father Lorane they can't quite figure out where sickle cell or the trait came from within his family. However, with sickle cell being hereditary someone down the line had the sickle cell disease for baby Cain to have sickle cell. While the research continues baby Cain doesn't seem to have many complications. The only crying he has done is the usual baby stuff including being hungry, sleep, using the bathroom, or even sometimes pain of some sort. The normal.

The vibes and commotion about baby Cain at the hospital is way different than the vibes at the Lorane house. The research continues along with the Lorane family typing up some information that's new to them or information they already knew, but thought was important to type for the future. The document went a little as so:

The Lorane Family
January 26th, 2095

Our baby boy Cain was born on Jan. 24th, 2095. At birth he was diagnosed with sickle cell anemia. We (the parents of Cain) have now realized that we both have the sickle cell trait and didn't know until now. Nothing changes with the love for our son, just wish we knew beforehand to maybe prevent putting our child through sickle cell.

Now with research we have found that sickle cell can cause multiple different problems temporarily and lifelong. We will do the best of our abilities to protect Cain and to give him all the love and support needed. Starting with the proper doctors, and sickle cell specialists available near us. With a great doctor team and the love/support from family we believe Cain will be healthy and the greatest at whatever he does or wants to do in life.

We both know and understand that we can't fully control what happens throuhout this fight with sickle cell, we can pray each and every day for his health and keep him uplifted. We understand now that his fight is now our fight!

-His fight is now Our fight!

Back at the hospital with an empty meeting room besides nurse Van and Bloodworth...

"I'm sorry, I didn't think it was you. I just had a lot going on mentally and didn't realize it was you and not Elaine."

(Bloodworth pauses before responding)

"It's fine I understand, I too have a lot going on, but I feel like we both are having the same problem."

"What makes you think that we have the same problem going on?" asked Van.

Hey like I said I think we should talk..." He looks around the room. "But not here."

As Van is still confused and worried about what happened with the baby she nervously answers with "Okay how about tomorrow before my shift because I'm exhausted and need to rest. This seems serious and I can't take any more stress or anything like that right now."

"Okay that is fine, what about the coffee shop around the corner because I also have work tonight, so we can go like an hour before our shifts."

"That's perfect enjoy your night."

"You do the same and get you some rest Van."

They both leave the meeting area after a long day and head home.

Once Van gets to her house, she throws her keys on the counter, then flops on the couch letting out a huge sigh. She immediately started thinking about baby Cain, and in the middle of her deep thoughts, she fell asleep without realizing. Sleeping all the way through the morning and day just about time for the meeting she had planned with Bloodworth.

She wakes up in full panic as it is now midday, and she has been sleeping on the couch for most of the day. She jumps up and hops in the shower to get ready for her shift and to meet up with Bloodworth at the coffee shop.

As for Bloodworth, he arrives at the coffee shop a little earlier than they planned.

"Hello welcome in how can we get your day started?" comes from behind the counter as Bloodworth walks in.

Bloodworth walks up to the counter "Umm... Yes, can I please just get a hot tea and an apple croissant."

Bloodworth goes on to pay for his items and gets a table waiting for items as well as waiting for nurse Van to arrive. As time goes by his name is called from behind the counter as his food and drink is ready.

It is now 30 minutes before the shift and he starts to think nurse Van isn't going to show, as he finishes his croissant, he gets up to throw the trash away and he hears the same voice from behind the counter again.

"Hello welcome in how can we get your day started?" It's nurse Van finally arriving.

He sits back down now waiting for Van to complete her order and join him.

Van approaches the counter "Yes can I get a caramel macchiato with a double shot of espresso, as well as one shot of espresso on the side."

Van finishes paying for her order and goes to join Bloodworth at the table.

"Hey Van, how are you this evening?" asked Bloodworth as she sat down with him.

"Phew extremely tired and not ready for work today. I had to order some extra energy today with the espresso"

"I understand that been there before. But yeah, it's getting close to clock in time so I'm going to jump straight to the point... The meeting earlier this morning. You kind of lashed out and asked some unusual things. What was that all about?"

"Oh, that was nothing I just like saying random things during meetings to see reactions from others. Especially when it's a guest speaker. That's all." Van nervously shifted around in her seat.

"Okay so let's be honest here." Bloodworth says as he sits up in his chair leaning into the table more. "We both know that's not true at all. That all seemed extremely personal like you had something built up in you. I'm going to start by saying what I need to say so maybe it will help you feel comfortable on telling me the truth on what that was about."

Van stares at him with a blank look not knowing what to say. As she has obviously been caught in a lie.

Bloodworth goes on to talk *"So the other night I had to check the blood bank to make sure the temperature reset to the correct temperature since the power had cut off hours prior..."*

As Van looks at him with deep concern now that he mentioned the power, the lady from behind the counter yells out *"Van your order is ready."*

Van quickly gets up, grabs her things from the counter and quickly sits back down as she is now invested in what Bloodworth has to say. *"You were saying?"*

"Yeah, after I walk in, I see in the discard section of the blood vial fridge something glowing"

Van throws the shot of espresso in her mouth and chases it with the macchiato.

Bloodworth looks at her with a concerning face, sips his tea and proceeds to tell his story *"I initially thought it was just a light reflection or something but then after I open the drawer I noticed a yellow glow to a blood vial."*

Van leans in closer while looking around and slowly whispers *"baby Cain"*

Bloodworth looks at her not knowing why she said that nor who baby Cain is.

Van gets up and says, *"We can't talk here!"* goes to the counter and orders another shot of espresso. It doesn't take as long just for an espresso shot, so she takes the shot, grabs her macchiato off the table and proceeds to walk out the door leaving Bloodworth sitting down in confusion.

Bloodworth finally collects his thoughts, grabs his tea and follows her out the door seconds later. He rushes out to find Van. He yells out as she is walking down the street towards the hospital *"Okay so where are we going to talk?"*

As Van continues to walk towards the hospital, he catches up to her and she goes on to say. *"Hey, listen the night the power went out something unusual happened to me. I was working on the pediatric side of the hospital, and we had to run test on a baby…"*

She continues her story about baby Cain and the situation she witnessed. At the end of her story Bloodworth asked, *"By chance I know we typically aren't supposed to discuss patients' health, but does he/she have sickle cell?"*

Van instantly stops walking, looks at Bloodworth and asks. *"How did you know that? I never mentioned that at all during the story."*

He explains to Van how he took the vial out for his own personal research and found an unnormal amount of Sickled shaped red blood cells. So many that he assumed the person was still admitted. He finishes with. *"We must keep all of this between us Van. WE could really get in trouble for all of this. Especially now dealing with a baby. This is too deep in with HIPAA."*

Van agrees and tells Bloodworth that Elaine knows but also that Elaine doesn't quite believe everything she has told her.

"Okay well let's leave it at that, just between us" as they continue to start walking towards the hospital again.

Van looks at Bloodworth and says *"You think we should get the vial of blood? We have already broken enough rules to get into the worst trouble possible. Might as well go for it all. It could help us and or that family in the future."*

Bloodworth looks at Van stating. *"I was thinking that yesterday way before the meeting. It could help us with future research, but at the same time it's the biggest risk ever."*

Van shrugs her shoulders and says. *"It's a huge risk, but we have already gone out of proper procedures plus I feel like the vial is better off in our hands considering we know what happened. Imagine that blood vial going off to a random lab,* starts glowing again or whatever may happen and then it comes back on the hospital, and they start a full investigation. We just have to be smart about who we let know and how we go about this in the future."

"Okay you might be right about that. Well, I will make it my plans to get the vial tonight and let's meet back at my house to get everything situated with this."

As Van and Bloodworth finally make it to the hospital she agrees with the plan and lets Bloodworth know to call her if he needs her during the shift. They finally walk through the doors and go to clock in to get the night shift started.

Van stands on her quote saying to herself. "I knew baby Cain was different."

Chapter 6

Chasing Shadows

It's finally Friday for the night shift. Only 4 days after the birth of baby Cain, it's been a long 4 days for nurse Van. This is finally the end of the week for a nice weekend. While clocking in for her shift Van is approached by nurse Elaine.

"Hey Van, how are you today? Sorry about last night I was just worried about you."

"No need for you to be sorry. I was just having a bad night and didn't want to talk about anything. I'm good though how are you?"

"Good, and I'm glad you're well. Let's get the night started! Last night until a well needed break." says Elaine as she walks away from Van.

As Van continues her clock in, she is thinking about how tonight will go and if it's potentially her last day on the job or not. Getting caught in such an act of "stealing" a blood vial sounds like instant termination and potentially legal issues leading to jail time. Van goes on with her shift hoping the night goes by fast enough to not worry all day.

As for Bloodworth, once he clocks in, he instantly walks to the blood bank fridge. He is checking everywhere for some sort of glow within the blood. Because blood is in and out so much its never in the same spot as before. He starts checking everywhere for the vial, but surprisingly enough it is not one vial within the fridge that gives off a glow. He slightly starts to panic and thinks it may be too late to secure the blood. After a few hours of on and off searching for the blood vial he decides to call nurse Van to inform her what's going on.

Vans nursing phone rings. "Hello this is nurse Van how can I help you?"

"Van it's me. We got to talk."

Van recognizing Bloodworth's voice over the phone she looks around the hall she was standing in at the time and whispers over the phone. "Oh. Hey, okay want to go to the meeting room?"

"No. Breakroom." The phone hangs up before she can respond.

Once they both arrive in the break room, they must act non-suspicious as they are not alone. Van can already see the concern on Bloodworths' face. They don't instantly start talking about the blood vial, instead Bloodworth calls out nurse Van's energy as she paces around the breakroom.

"Hey Van, are you okay? Looks like that caffeine from earlier is got you on high energy."

Van answers knowing its more nervous energy than actual energy. "Oh yeah it really does. I shouldn't have taken those two extra shots of espresso down at the coffee shop."

Bloodworth opens the fridge and grabs two bottles of water. He walks over towards Van as she is in the back away from everyone else now.

As he hands Van the water he whispers to her. "I think the vial is gone." Making Van get strangled on the water.

She gets herself together and finally asks. "Are you sure?"

"Well, I'm not 1,000% sure but I couldn't find anything actually glowing."

Van sips more water and ask, "*Did you not write down or remember the discharge number on the vial?*"

Bloodworth stops and looks at Van. "*How do you know about the discharge numbers on the blood vial?*"

"*Come on now. I've worked here 30 plus odd years I know a little more than you think I do about the ends and outs of this hospital.*"

Van finishes her water walks to the trash can being followed by Bloodworth. She turns around and whispers. "*It's a slight. Very slight window between shift changes I can come by and help you go through all the vials in between the change.*"

"*Okay sounds good. I will do what I can to search some more while I finish up my shift as well.*"

They both walk out of the breakroom and off to finish their shift.

At the Lorane family's house there still isn't much commotion while dealing with baby Cain and his sickle cell. He is still living a "normal" healthy baby life. Despite the mishap of the microwave going out it has all been normal. The family didn't realize that baby Cain was the reason behind that.

While heating up baby Cains bottle, he let out a huge cry that didn't last very long. In fact, it didn't even last long enough for the Lorane's to even react in time before he quit crying. The cry ended up sending an electrical current throughout the house and causing the microwave to trip. Maybe it was some sort of electrical discharge from baby Cain. Possibly the end of his unknown abilities.

While baby Cain has now let out what could have been his last electrical surge, and the Lorane family attempts to fix the microwave; Bloodworth is still working on finding the vial.

It is now close to not only shift change, but that little window of time is slowly creeping up. Bloodworth now has to figure out how to hold down the blood bank and wait for Van to make sure no one sees them looking for the blood vial.

Van finished all her work and made sure every patient was set early. For the last five minutes of her shift, she has been watching the clock nonstop. The time between shifts is going to determine their success in this. As the clock hits 7am Van clocks out instantly grabs her belongings and heads off to the blood bank to meet up with Bloodworth.

"Hey Van!" Elaine yells from down the hall as Van steps into the elevator.

Shoot do I wait or just leave her. Van asked herself.

Van ends up waiting for Elaine to get in the elevator. *"Hey Van glad you waited. I just wanted to check on you to make sure you're good and had a good day of work today. Haven't seen much of you today besides when we first clocked in."*

"Yes, I'm good just been a busy day. Glad to be off and go home for the weekend. Today was my last day for the week."

Elaine looks up and realizes the elevator numbers are moving up instead of to the ground floor parking garage.

"Van, you realize its going up and not to the parking garage?"

Van looks up and then back to Elaine quickly coming up with a lie. *"Yeah, I have to drop some paperwork off for someone first."*

Elaine doesn't second guess the situation and tells Van to call her once she gets home to go out for dinner potentially. Van steps off the elevator at the same time of hitting the "G" on the elevator ensuring Elaine goes to the ground floor.

"Okay I will call you later on." Van says as the elevator doors close.

Van now makes her way towards the blood bank in hopes of no more distractions or interruptions. At the same time of hoping they don't get caught by anyone.

In the blood bank Bloodworth's relief arrives already closing the window of time that Van was speaking of. Quick thinking Bloodworth sends his relief out on a mission in hopes of having enough time to get Van in to help find the blood vial. As the relief walks out of the office Bloodworth gets up and walks into the blood bank fridge.

Van and the relief end up bumping into each other in the hallway. Van with her head down trying not to make conversations with anyone to get to the blood bank office successfully. Even though her head was down the relief still questions Van.

"Excuse me. Sorry to bother you, but do you by chance know where I can find the science lab? I'm a send over from a different hospital and just don't know my way around just yet."

As Van looked up, she was going to answer truthfully with "Science lab? That's not a thing here yet." But she notices his name badge had on it "Blood Bank Physician" She quickly puts two and two together and realizes she needs to lie because she doesn't want him to end up back in the office.

While looking up from the badge she answers *"I believe they are doing construction on the first-floor elevator to finish the science lab. If it is open already you will have to take the elevator to the second floor, then take the steps to the first* floor." Without hesitation the blood bank physician says okay and walks towards the elevator.

Van now scurries towards the blood bank office and through the doors of the fridge scaring Bloodworth. Bloodworth jumps and looks towards the door.

"Oh, Van it's just you!? You scared me."

Van drops her things. "Let's hurry before your little buddy realizes the science lab isn't a thing here yet."

Bloodworth looks up at Van with a smirk. "How do you know about that? Why do you know so much that's going on around this hospital?"

"I ran into him in the hallway and had to quickly come up with my second lie in less than two minutes. Anyways where should I start?"

Bloodworth points towards the back of the fridge wall. "Start over there and go around that way we will meet in the middle. Or we won't. hopefully we find it before then."

A quick three minutes go by while looking for the vial. Van and Bloodworth are running out of patients as well as running out of time before the relief comes back for his shift. Van opens the last draw on the back wall and notices a vial not glowing, but putting off a different unique color compared to the other vials around it. Van puts on gloves and slowly picks up the blood vial.

Van slowly brings the vial closer to her face to read the label. *"Did you ever find the discard numbers, or are we just out looking for a random vial of glowing blood?"*

"Ahh we are just full of jokes today huh?" Bloodworth lets out a slight chuckle while proceeding to call out. *"0420BB1995"*

Van slowly stands up with the vial in her hand and freaking out. *"I...I...I got it"*

Bloodworth quickly closes the doors of the fridge and walks over to Van grabbing the vial away from her.

"Van now isn't the time to freeze up like this, get out of here before my relief comes back and finds you in here. Go home freshen up and we will talk about this later when it is clear."

Van realizes he is right and quickly snaps out of it, grabs her things and heads off to the elevators.

Bloodworth quickly packs up his things, safely puts the vial in some styrofoam to keep the temperature regulated and safe from breaking. The other physician finally makes his way back up and into the office.

"Hey, the science lab is not open yet apparently and I also couldn't find any location or discarded blood vials out on file."

"That's okay. I appreciate you going to check while I finish up here. I ended up finishing earlier

than expected and already clocked out. I was just waiting for you to get back before leaving. Quickly before I go though, the power in this hospital has been acting up lately so just make sure you keep an eye on the temperature in the blood bank, it could reset."

Bloodworth closes his laptop and heads out of the office to finally go home after the longest day ever. Once outside and in his car, he calls up Van.

"Hey, I got out with the blood vial with no problems from anyone."

"Okay good this is only the beginning I'm afraid."

"Yeah, you're right. Only the beginning... I guess this makes us a team!"

The phone call ends.

Chapter 7

<u>Beyond the Pain</u>

- Sixteen Years Later -

It's been quite some time. Sixteen years for some have felt long, while for others, it's gone by quickly. For Cain, he's not much of a baby anymore. Throughout his childhood, he fought sickle cell. But he adopted a mindset: "I have sickle cell; sickle cell doesn't have me." And that attitude has never let it stop him from doing anything he set his mind to. Sickle cell isn't an easy battle, but the strength of a warrior makes it look easy.

The Lorane family stuck to their motto: "His fight is now our fight." They did everything they could to raise Cain in the best way possible. Over the years, they found an amazing sickle cell specialist, who's been helping Cain since he was one year old. His parents kept pushing him to believe in being "normal." Cain played sports growing up, including t-ball and basketball. Despite having sickle cell, he didn't let it make him any less "ordinary." But dealing with sickle cell was what set him apart.

Cain's episodes and pain crises didn't start affecting him until he was about 10 years old. All tests and blood work came back "normal" for Cain, especially compared to the very first vial of blood when he was born. In fact, doctors even questioned whether he had sickle cell, considering how smoothly things had gone for the first decade of his life. They even wondered if maybe he was the "cure" that scientists had been looking for. The Loranes always viewed Cain as a blessing, so they never second-guessed his fight. But the truth is, it was the storm that raged from the beginning that kept Cain so "healthy" and out of the ordinary in his battle with sickle cell.

It took 10 years for the storm to settle, and the sickling took over. From ages 10 and up, the fight became the usual for a warrior: pain, fatigue, hospital visits, and appointments. Cain's battles mostly involved pain in his chest, back, and legs. Every warrior's pain is unique, though.

In his younger years, Cain always questioned his life and why he seemed so "different" from his peers. But when sickle cell started affecting him more, he didn't really question it. It wasn't until middle school, around the age of 12-13, that he began to realize he wasn't quite like everyone else. "Why am I going through all of this? Why can't I play in the cold like my friends, before I start hurting or end up in the hospital? Why do I have to go to the hospital just to control my pain? Am I weak? Is something wrong with me? Will I ever live a normal life like my friends?"

These are heavy questions for a child to carry. And they're just the beginning of what a sickle cell warrior goes through mentally. It's a part of what makes us warriors—the never-ending mental and physical fight. It took a lot of courage for Cain, but eventually, he asked his parents why he wasn't as "normal" as his friends, and why he couldn't do the things they did as often.

They explained what sickle cell was, the complications it could cause, and the reasons behind the pain. The Loranes also emphasized that he was normal and shouldn't feel different.

"Cain, you can do and become anything you want in this world. Sickle cell doesn't define you." His parents always told him. That conversation stuck with Cain, and whenever he felt down, he would remember those words.

Now, at 15 years old, Cain is about to enter his sophomore year in high school. His freshman year was rough, to say the least. In fact, it was one of the hardest years he had in dealing with sickle cell. The first year of high school is stressful enough for any kid, but imagine that combined with the fight against sickle cell, and the pressure of maintaining good grades to graduate.

Freshman year brought Cain to his lowest point. Doctors would say he was lucky to be alive, but his family believes he's blessed. Cain, though, relies on the warrior within him to keep fighting—to prove the doctors and scientists wrong in everything he does. During his freshman year, Cain spent a significant amount of time in the hospital. He dealt with intense chest pain that led to acute chest syndrome and pneumonia. On top of that, his hemoglobin and blood pressure were fluctuating.

Over the course of his hospital stays, Cain received eight units of blood through transfusions, often given every other day. There were times when Cain thought about giving up. Mentally exhausted and overwhelmed by the pain, he reached a breaking point. But in those moments, he remembered that he was stronger than sickle cell, and he pushed forward.

Now, at 15 years old, Cain is gearing up for his sophomore year. His freshman year was one of the hardest, filled with challenges both physical and emotional. High school is tough for any kid, but Cain had to battle more than just tests and homework. He fought through pain, hospital visits, and the pressure to stay strong—inside and out. It's not an easy road, but Cain has learned that true strength doesn't always mean pushing through without pain. Sometimes, it's about accepting the fight, the setbacks, and the moments of doubt, and still choosing to keep going.

As he heads into his sophomore year, Cain isn't just facing the next chapter of high school—he's facing the future with more hope, more determination, and a warrior's heart that won't stop fighting. He's not done yet. His fight continues, and with every step, he's showing the world that no matter what comes next, he's ready.

Chapter 8

<u>Buried Secrets</u>

A voice cut through the silence *"Excuse me, ma'am. Ma'am!"*
The voice gets louder. *"What you're doing is illegal. I need you to leave now, or I'll call security."* Silence fills the room again, time stretching on.

About 30 minutes pass before another voice breaks the stillness. *"FREEZE! Don't touch that!"*

Van jumps up, throwing her covers off, panicking and waking up in a cold sweat. She quickly realizes she's heavily breathing, realizing it was only a dream. She reaches over to her nightstand, grabs a half-empty water bottle, and chugs it.

Finally, she calms herself down and gets out of bed to go to the bathroom. Van splashes water on her face and stares at her reflection in the mirror.

Still out of breath, she mutters under her breath, "*I can't believe it's been 16 years, and I'm still having different dreams about what could've happened and what did happen. I need to get it together.*"

It's been a long 16 years for nurse Van. Nightmares—memories, really—about baby Cain still haunt her. Despite being retired for the last 11 years, she hasn't been able to shake the flashbacks. After 35 years of working at the hospital, she decided to step away and finally enjoy life. But she can't help but wonder what happened to Cain, if his life turned out as extraordinary as she once thought.

After pulling herself together, Van picks up the phone and dials Bloodworth. Unlike Van, Bloodworth is still working at the hospital, and now he's one of the head honchos in charge of the blood bank. Things are going well for him, and no one has questioned the missing blood vial from that night. If only he could get Van to let it go and accept that no one will ever find out.

Bzzz...bzzz...bzzzzzz

Bloodworth answers the phone. "*Hello, this is—*"

Van interrupts. *"Hey, it's just Van. I know we're still keeping logs and doing investigations on 'patient Sickled Shock.' I wanted to let you know I had another one of those dreams."*

– Patient "Sickled Shock" or Patient SS refers to Cain Lorane. It's the name they came up with over the 16 years, used to keep his identity hidden just in case word ever got out about what Van and Bloodworth know. "Sickled" comes from the sickle cell Bloodworth discovered in the vial, and "Shock" is based on Van's experience that night. –

"Oh, wow. Really? It's been at least once a month now, hasn't it?"

"Yeah, I'm not sure what's going on, but I have a feeling it won't stop until we figure out everything about Patient Sickled Shock."

"It'll all work out, trust me, Van. Plus, it's been 16 years and no one at the office has even mentioned it."

"Funny you say that. This dream was about me getting caught taking the blood vial from the blood bank fridge."

"Van, listen, I've got to get back to work. We'll talk more later, okay?"

Van looks at the clock. "*Oh, wow, sorry, I didn't even realize what time it was. Let's talk later. Sorry about that—have a good day.*"

The phone hangs up.

As the call ends, Bloodworth pulls out a notebook from his bag and writes:

August 20th, 2111

Quick log: Van had another dream about Patient Sickled Shock and about the night in 2095 when the vial "went missing."

He closes the journal, puts it back in his bag, and goes back to work.

Once the phone call with Bloodworth ends, Van dials Elaine next. Elaine retired as a nurse and now works part-time as a supervisor at Portsville Pharmacy. It's not just any part-time job—she's in charge of the pharmacy, and her years of experience as a nurse help her run things smoothly. Though Elaine stepped away from nursing to enjoy life, she took the supervisor position as a way to stay involved without committing full-time.

Elaine answers the phone with a smile in her voice. "*Hello, thanks for calling Portsville Phamily Pharmacy. How can we help you today?*"

"*Hey Elaine, it's Van. Just checking in on you and my prescriptions.*"

Elaine's smile grows wider at the sound of Van's voice. *"Oh, hey Van! I've been good. It's great to hear from you. I've been told by different coworkers that you ask about me every time you come in for your medicine. How's the retired life treating you?"*

Elaine starts typing up Van's information on the computer to check if her prescriptions are ready.

"I'm living, you know. Staying strong and taking it day by day. Can't complain."

Van's not one to complain, always keeping things to herself.

Elaine chuckles. *"Well, that's good to hear. I'm pulling up your info now. Do you miss it? Miss being a nurse?"*

"Actually, yeah, but I love the time off. I go visit the hospital sometimes just to get that feeling again, but not sure if I miss it enough to come back." The two share a light chuckle.

"You should join me at the pharmacy. It'd be like old times!" Elaine laughs.

"Yeah? Maybe. Who knows? Could be something for the future."

"Just think about it. Okay, so it looks like all four of your prescriptions are ready. Insulin, potassium, tramadol, and cis..." Elaine pauses, a slight worry creeping into her voice. *"Cisplatin?"*

The phone call goes silent for a moment.

"...Van?" Elaine clears her throat. "Van, do you... have cancer?"

The silence stretches out.

Van breaks it, her voice flat. "Enough with all that. I'll come by to pick up my medication later. Thanks for confirming the prescriptions are ready."

The phone hangs up, leaving Elaine alone in the pharmacy, hurt, confused, and worried about Van.

- Looks like Van and Elaine haven't been talking much since retirement. Seems like some rekindling is needed. I told you—it's been a long 16 years for some, and a quick 16 years for others. -

Chapter 9

The Calm Before the Storm

Cain sat, staring out of his bedroom window, watching the bright sun reflect off the cars driving by the house. It was the last weekend before he started his sophomore year of high school, and he couldn't help but reflect on how his freshman year went. He hoped that this year wouldn't be anything like the last. Sickle cell has its own way of causing PTSD in warriors. The memories of past pain crises could trigger stress and anxiety, and right now, that anxiety was making him overthink the upcoming year of classes.

Cain slid off his bed and onto his knees, closing his eyes as he began to pray.

"Dear Lord, I come to you right now with open arms. I want to start by saying thank you for all that you do and have done. Thank you for keeping me strong through my fight, Lord. I know—no, we know—sickle cell isn't an easy battle. But with you by my side, I know I can get through anything. I trust that you wouldn't have given me this fight if you didn't believe I could win it. So, Lord, I ask that you watch over me and let this sophomore year be smoother than last. Please keep me as healthy and as strong as possible. In Jesus' name, I pray. Amen."

Cain wiped away a tear and stood up, taking a deep breath. He was ready to face the last weekend before school started on Monday.

As he was getting dressed, Cain heard his mother talking to someone downstairs. He turned the water off from the sink.

"I believe he's upstairs getting dressed now. I'll let him know," his mom's voice came through the floorboards.

Cain finished brushing his teeth, threw on his shirt, and headed downstairs.

"Cain!" His mother called out.

"Yes, ma'am!" Cain stumbled down the stairs.

"Dexter just came by. He said he'll be waiting for you down the street. How are you feeling this morning?"

"Oh, okay. I'll head out and meet him. I'm good, though, Mom. Hope you're doing well too. Love you."

Cain hugged his mom and grabbed the last pastry from the box, tossing it in the trash on his way out the door.

Before he could close the door behind him, his mom stopped him. "Cain, this is your last weekend before school starts. Don't overdo it. You know how your body is. And don't let Dexter get you into any trouble," she added with a smirk.

Cain walks back into the house, added, "Yeah, Mom, you're right. I won't do too much today." Grabs a water form the fridge and proceeds back out the door, closing it behind him.

Seconds later Cain opened the door again, looking at his mom with a grin. "And you know Dexter is the last one to get anyone into trouble." He closed the door, leaving his mom laughing.

Dexter Bridges and Cain had grown up together. Dexter was the quiet type—always to himself, never picking fights, and definitely not one to stir up trouble. They were neighborhood best friends, a bond forged over years. Dexter had seen Cain at his highest and his lowest, especially when sickle cell made life difficult. Though Dexter didn't understand sickle cell completely, he never questioned it until last year, when he witnessed firsthand everything Cain went through. Dexter was at the hospital every day he could after school, always wanting to see his friend healthy and happy. He'd noticed how hard it was for the hospital to manage Cain's pain. It was then that Dexter decided to put his tech skills to work, trying to create something that might help Cain.

"Yo, Dex! What's up, bro?" Cain called out as he approached Dexter.

The two dap each other up.

"Not much, man. How you feeling today?" Dexter asked.

"Ah, you know, I'm go—" Cain started, but Dexter interrupted him.

"Yeah, I know, I know. Don't say 'I'm good,' because I already know how you are when someone asks you that. How are you really feeling today bro?"

They both laugh.

Sickle cell warriors typically blow off the question of 'how are you doing?' with the simple answer of fine, good, or doing alright and forcing the question back on to whoever asked. It's a hard question as a warrior to answer because we don't want to always seem as if we are complaining about our well-being in that moment. With Cain being the warrior he is he attempted to blow Dexters question to the side. However with Dexter being his close friend he knows how Cain will answer and forces him to explain more on how he is actually feeling.

"Nah, I'm actually good today, just a little stressed about the new school year coming up on Monday." Cain answers with a slight gilt look on his face.

"Yeah, I can only imagine after everything you went through last year," Dexter said. "But hey, that's behind you now. This year will be different, I know it. And trust me, I'll find a way to help with my tech brain. Just wait."

"Yeah, you're right. We'll see. I definitely appreciate you, bro."

"Of course. Now let's go shoot some hoops for a bit." Dexter tossed the ball to Cain.

The two played basketball for about 30 minutes, but Dexter stopped, knowing Cain would push himself too far if left unchecked. He could see it in Cain's face—he was overdoing it.

"Yo, Cain, your floater's looking pretty good. Who do you think you are?" Dexter joked.

They both laughed.

"Not sure, just started trying things out. Why'd you stop though?"

"*Just a little tired, that's all,*" Dexter lied, covering for his friend.

"*Oh, okay, that's fine. I'm a little exhausted myself,*" Cain replied, knowing Dexter was just looking out for him.

The two sat down on the curb, catching their breath.

Cain took a sip of his water and turned to Dexter. "*So, you ready for this year?*"

"*Yeah, I am. Ready to see all our friends and meet our new classmates. I know you said you were stressing about sophomore year, but aren't you looking forward to getting back to school? You missed the end of last year, after all.*"

"*Yeah, I am,*" Cain said. "*And I know I said I'm stressing, but I've got this strange feeling that things are going to change for me this year... Or maybe for us.*"

"*What do you mean by that, Cain?*" Dexter asked, glancing over at him.

Cain laid back on the grass, staring up at the sky. "*I'm not sure. Honestly, I just feel like something's off... It could be nerves, but I don't know. I just have this feeling something will happen this year. In a good way, though.*"

"*Yeah, maybe it's just nerves,*" Dexter said, standing up and offering his hand to Cain. "*But let's head home and rest. I don't know about you, but*

I've gotta get mentally ready to start waking up early again."

Cain exhaled and grabbed Dexter's hand to help pull himself up. "*Let's do it!*" he said.

Little did they know, it wasn't just nerves Cain was feeling.

Chapter 10

The Calm Before the Hunt

Van stared at the phone after the call ended, her hand slightly shaking. She'd brushed past Elaine's question, but the weight of it lingered in the air. Cancer. The word just repeated in her mind over and over again. Van hadn't told anyone—not even Elaine—about the diagnosis. Not that it was a secret, but she was afraid to face the reality of it all. Afraid of what it actually meant.

On the other end, Elaine was questioning herself. Is it my fault we've been so distant lately? Am I a terrible friend? Why didn't she tell me? These questions flooded her mind, but she pushed them aside, trying to focus on work with customers waiting.

A little over an hour later, Van arrived to pick up her medicine. Elaine, so focused on her work, didn't even realize who was waiting.

"*Next in line, please!*" Elaine called, walking to the front desk.

Van stepped up to the counter, silently waiting. Elaine looked up and was surprised to see her.

"*Van! Oh my, it's so good to see you!*" Elaine walked from behind the counter and gave Van a hug. "*I'm sorry I haven't been much of a friend lately, and I'm sorry you're going through this. Just know I'm 100% here for you now and the rest of the way. I'm sorry, Van!*"

The hug broke, and Van grabbed Elaine's arms, holding her hands. "*It's okay. You did nothing wrong. Once I found out, I didn't tell anyone and focused on getting myself healthy. The doctors say we caught it early, and I should be fine after a few more treatments.*"

"*More? So, you've already gone through—*" Elaine started.

Van leaned in, looking around at the other customers in the pharmacy. "*Hey, Elaine, I'll be fine. I promise. You've got customers to take care of, so get back there and get my medicine.*"

They both chuckled as Van joked.

"Okay, fine, but I'll be calling you tonight. We have to catch up," Elaine said, heading back through the doors.

Elaine grabbed Van's medicine from the bin and rang her up. As Van paid and left the pharmacy.

Later that night, it was well past the time Bloodworth would usually get off work. Once home and settled in, he went over plans by himself before calling Van. He pulled out his notebook from earlier, labeled "Blood Vials & Patients" across the cover. Flipping through the pages—mostly filled with notes on patients with sickle cell, Vans' dreams, and other tidbits—he reached a blank page and stared at it. Lying back on the couch, he gazed up at the ceiling. Will we ever figure this all out? he thought to himself, letting out a heavy sigh.

Bang! Bang! Bang!

Suddenly, the door shook violently with each knock, startling Bloodworth to his feet. The banging stopped for a moment, followed by a voice from behind the door.

"Hey, Sam, it's me. I hope you're okay in there. Hellooo!"

Bloodworth, standing in his living room with a look of confusion, realized it sounded like Van. He glanced over at the clock. Oh, it is Van.

"Coming!" he called as he walked to the door.

He opened it to find Van standing there with a worried look on her face.

"Well, hey, Bloodworth," Van said.

"Uh, hey, sorry, I must've fallen asleep on the couch. You look worried—everything okay?" he asked, stepping back into the house and leaving the door open for her to come in.

"Yeah, are you okay, is the question?" Van responded.

Bloodworth walked toward the kitchen. *"Yeah, I guess I just fell asleep after work. Not sure what happened, honestly,"* he chuckled.

Van closed the door behind her. *"Yeah, I texted you and called you before coming over. I thought something was wrong with you. Glad you answered the door after two minutes of knocking, though."* She laughed.

"Oh, yeah. I was knocked out," he said, glancing at his phone to see multiple unread messages and missed calls. *"Sorry about that. So, what's up?"*

"Not much at all, really," Van said, again avoiding bringing up her cancer.

"I wanted to talk about locking down and finding some sort of trace or identity for patient Sickled Shock. It's been 16 years, and that little baby haunts me in my sleep. I just want to know he's fine and living a successful life."

Bloodworth sat on the couch, handing Van a bottle of water. He flipped through his notebook, stopping on a page labeled "0420BB1995" Taking a pen, he crossed out the numbers and replaced them with "Patient Sickled Shock" Van noticed the number and remembered it being the label on the blood vial from years ago.

"Hey, what ever happened to that vial of blood we took, anyway?" Van asked.

Bloodworth quickly looked at her, opened his bottle of water, and took a quick sip, avoiding the question.

"Oh, it's not around anymore. So, about patient Sickled Shock..." he brushed off.

Van stared at him with an aggravated look. She felt like he was lying, but she didn't question it. She already had enough on her plate.

"Yeah, so... he should be around 15 or 16 now," she said. "Of course, I don't remember the exact date, but he should be at least that old."

Bloodworth responded with a dark look. "If he's still alive, that is."

Van sank deeper into the couch.

Suddenly, a bright flash of light illuminated the entire house, causing Van to sit up. Bloodworth also looked around.

"Did you—"

A loud thunderous crack interrupted her. The thunder grew constant, followed by more flashes of light. Van raised an eyebrow, then tilted her head slightly toward Bloodworth.

"Listen, call me crazy, but this has been the worst sounding thunderstorm in years. It's random, too. I don't remember anyone saying anything about rain or thunderstorms. Again, call me crazy, but if finding patient Sickled Shock was possible, now seems like an ironic time for him to show up— or for us to find him."

Bloodworth stared at Van. *"You are crazy. He doesn't just spawn from a thunderstorm like in a TV show."*

They both laughed.

"Well, I guess I'm crazy too," Bloodworth said, *"because you could be right. If anything happens, or if something shows up, we have no choice but to drop everything and meet up. This is the week we find a trace."*

Van got up, heading for the door. *"Patient Sickled Shock, I hope you're well,"* she said, leaving Bloodworth's house.

The storm continued through the night, ending the weekend with an eerie feeling of anticipation.

Chapter 11

<u>Starting Strong</u>

Beep. Beep. Beep.

Cain stretches out long and grabs the cover, pulling it over his head to silence the alarm going off in his room.

Beep. Beep. Beep.

Cain shoots out his arm, slamming his hand on the snooze button. About 10 minutes go by.

Beep. Beep. Beep.

Cain groans, "Okay, okay, I'm up," slamming the alarm again while rolling over to sit on the side of the bed. *Well, the day is finally here. The start of my sophomore year.*

"Cain!" his father yells from the other side of the door.

"Yes, sir, I'm up!" Cain responds while dropping to his knees to pray.

Cain has always taken his time to pray about any of his situations. He truly believes that he is a blessing, given the fight of sickle cell for a reason. He believes that everything happens for a reason, and his fight must continue to find its purpose.

Once he finishes his prayer, he gets up, gets dressed, and starts his day. Downstairs, he sees that his mom had cooked breakfast before leaving for work. She made bacon, eggs, grits, and heated up some leftover pork chops. While Cain wasn't much of a breakfast eater, he settles for a bowl of cereal. On his way out the door, he grabs a piece of bacon and heads off to the bus stop.

At the bus stop, Dex is already waiting for Cain. As Cain approaches, he holds out his hand and daps up Dex.

"Was good, Dex?"

"Not much, bro. Happy to see you back at the stop. It's been a while seeing you actually here. Not gonna lie, when you're in the hospital, I don't know what to do with myself."

"Yeah, feels good to be back. Hopefully, it won't be the last."

"Don't even put that in the air, man. You'll be just fine my friend."

Cain laughs, looking at Dex. "Ay, man, I haven't been gone that long, have I? You losing your lingo already? What's up with you saying, 'my friend'?"

Cain and Dex both burst out laughing.

"My bad. It's been a long break," Dex responds as the bus finally pulls up to the stop.

The bus pulls to a screeching stop with the sound of steam shortly after, and the doors open. Dex steps on first, followed by Cain. The chants and cheers are loud, welcoming Cain back to school.

"Woooo! Cain is back! Cain's on the bus! Wassup, Cain? Woooo!" Even the bus driver welcomes Cain back.

The cheers die down, and Cain and Dex sit next to each other on the way to school.

"Well, well. Someone is popular and well-missed," Dex says, nudging Cain with his elbow.

"Hey, what can I say? You know I bring the life to the bus." They both start laughing. "I know who doesn't miss me or cares to see my face. At least I don't care to see them."

Dex looks at Cain. "Right. Tony Simmons, and Brixton Steele."

Tony Simmons and Brixton Steele, aka Breezy, are known as the school bullies or enemies of the school. They're sneaky with everything they do.

None of the teachers ever catch them in the act, and they rarely get into trouble. All the students dislike them. They pick fights with anyone. For some reason, they really have it out for Cain. No one has had the guts to stand up to them yet, but this year things might be different.

"Maan, forget those dudes. One day, somebody's gonna stand up for themselves, and they're gonna regret what they do. Shoot, maybe I will stand up to them one day."

"*Cap!*" Cain says, and they both start laughing. "*Nah, you're right about them picking the wrong fight one day, but you're not standing up to anyone, Dex. Let's be honest here.*" Cain gives Dex a nudge.

"*That's messed up, Cain. We'll see though.*"

Once they arrive at school, they meet up with their other friends before classes start. Cain gets love and support from all his friends after missing the end of his freshman year. Breaking up the huddle of Dex and Cain's group comes Tony and Breezy. The two of them approach Cain through the small circle. Dex side-eyes Cain while listening to the conversation.

"*Well, well, well. Look who it is, Tony. Nice of you to join us again, Cain.*" Breezy says as Tony walks over to Cain.

"*Where have you been?*" Tony asks at the same time as grabbing Cain's wrist. "*I see you didn't gain any weight over your little vacation.*"

Breezy laughs at the joke. Cain snatches his arm away.

"*Look, it's a new year, new everything. We're sophomores now. Chill with the kid stuff.*"

Dex raises his eyebrows in shock. Tony and Breezy look at each other and then around at the small crowd.

"*You...*" Tony starts to talk at the same time, being interrupted by Breezy.

"*You talking to us?*" Breezy says. Both Tony and Breezy start laughing.

"*Tony, you hear this guy?*"

Beeeeeep!

Everyone looks up at the clock. That was the first bell, signaling that class starts in two minutes. At this point, everyone walks away from the circle, and others head to class.

Breezy puts his shoulder in Cain's chest and whispers in his ear. "*Listen, punk, we run this school. Don't forget that. We aren't scared of you.*" He walks through Cain, looking back at Tony, giving him a head nod to move out. Tony also bumps into Cain and Dex following Breezy.

Dex and Cain walk away.

Cain looks at Dex while they walk to class. "What happened, Mr. 'I'll stand up to them'?"

"You called cap, ain't that how that works?" Dex asks, as they both walk into the same classroom, laughing at the situation.

"Wait, you have science class first block too?"

"Yeah, what, you think I'm walking you to class or something?" Dex laughs.

"Oh, Dex is full of jokes this year, I see." They both sit in the back of the classroom.

Beeeeeep!

The final bell rings. The teacher walks into the classroom and closes the door behind him.

"Hello, class. My name is Mr. Watson."

- **Clark Watson that is.** -

Chapter 12

The Science of Us

Clark Watson, now known as Mr. Watson to the students of Portsville High School, has come a long way. Clark Watson was the professor/doctor who gave the speech at the hospital during the meeting years ago. His main goal from the beginning was to become a teacher while also earning his doctor's degree and specializing in sickle cell anemia. Let's just say his 16 years went exactly as planned, with a few speed bumps along the way. Now, he's here at Portsville High, teaching. Teaching Cain, at that. It's all slowly coming full circle.

"Hello class, my name is Mr. Watson. I will be your science teacher for the semester."

What started off as loud enthusiasm, he now lowers his voice to say, "Between me and all of you here, I'm the coolest teacher in the building," making the class laugh at his personality.

Cain looks at Dex and smiles. "This should be a fun class," he says.

"I will be your human biology and health science teacher. Here, you will learn a lot about the human body and how our bodies work. You'll learn how we fight off different things and how we're all superheroes in our own way. I always told my mother I wanted to be a superhero when I was growing up. Well, here I am." He places his hands on his hips, standing in a hero stance, making the class laugh.

"But anyways, like I said, I'm the cool teacher, so we aren't going to start class with the traditional 'stand up, say your name, and do two truths and a lie.' Instead, I'll tell you a little bit about my health and life. Since this is a health science class, I'll then give anyone the floor if they want to share something about themselves. However, it's up to you guys to get to know each other as the semester goes on. We got a deal here?"

The class responds, "Yes, yeah, yes sir."

"Okay, so just really quick, so I can tell you what's planned for the week. Two years ago, around this time, I was having extreme difficulties with my heart and was honestly heading in the wrong direction. Long story short, I was blessed enough to go through a full heart transplant and strong enough to prove many doctors wrong. Now I'm here today, in front of all of you, doing my dream job of teaching. I say that to say this: Don't let someone tell you 'you can't,' especially someone in the medical field. I can say that because I graduated in the medical field with my doctorate. We are trained and..."

A student raises their hand in the middle of Clark Watson's speech.

"Yes?" Mr. Watson says, pointing at the student.

"Mr. Watson, if you have your PhD, why are you here?"

"Well, my dream is to teach. My passion is to help others as a doctor and to learn more about the medical field. Plus, I get to help and teach you guys things I didn't learn in school but learned hands-on in the field." He looks at the student.

"Okay, that makes sense. Thanks for answering that."

"So, as I was saying, don't let someone tell you 'you can't.' Doctors and nurses are trained to read a 'script,' if you will. They just read notes, charts, and things they have learned. Don't let them tell you what you can and can't do. Your body is the ultimate authority. Now, would anyone else like to get up and tell a story or share something about their health? Again, this isn't for a grade or anything, so don't feel like you have to answer."

Cain and Dex look at each other. Dex gives Cain a subtle head tilt, trying to get him to speak.

Another student gets up. "Umm, I broke my ankle while skateboarding once."

Mr. Watson chuckles to himself as the class laughs. "Okay, nice to know. Way to break the ice with that. No pun intended. Anyone else?"

Again, Dex looks at Cain. He leans over and says, "Come on, bro. Now's your chance—not only to spread awareness, but to let everyone know what's been going on with you."

Cain sits back in his chair, thinking about the moment. Finally, he decides to stand up.

"Okay, great. You can either come up or tell it from there."

Cain decides to stay where he is instead of going to the front of the class.

"Hey, what's up, class and friends? Some of you know me already, and if not, my name's Cain. You may know that I missed most of the end of freshman year. I'm a warrior of sickle cell anemia."

Mr. Watson slowly puts down the coffee mug he was drinking from, now fully invested in Cain's story, since he specializes in sickle cell. Cain continues.

"*Sickle cell is a blood disease that affects my red blood cells. Anyway, I don't want to take up the entire class, but yeah, that's it. I have sickle cell.*"

Cain sits back down. As he does, he notices everyone either searching the topic online or talking amongst themselves. He even hears one student say to another student, "*That's crazy, my grandmother had sickle cell.*"

Cain looks at Dex and shrugs. "*I did it.*"

"*Yeah, I could tell you were mad nervous, too. But hey, you got the class interested, though.*"

Cain chuckles. "*Bro, did you just say 'mad nervous'?*"

"*Yeah, just trying to get the lingo back, you know? Since you called me out on it earlier.*"

The two start laughing.

Meanwhile, Mr. Watson is sitting back, watching how the majority of the students are deeply engaged by Cain's story. He also takes note of how close Cain and Dex seem to be.

After letting the class chat for a couple of minutes, Mr. Watson finally speaks.

"Okay, okay, class. Attention, please. Cain, thank you for your story. Would anyone else like to share anything?"

All the students look around the room at each other, waiting for someone else to go next.

"Okay, well, thanks to those who shared. Now, I was going to go over the rubric and talk about what the next class will be like, but we'll hold off on that for now. I might take a different approach."

Class continues throughout the day. They cover grades, testing, homework—the usual first-day topics. It wasn't a hard day, but it was filled with information.

Beeeeeep!

The sound of the bell interrupts the class. Students start packing up their notebooks and preparing to leave.

"Okay, class, that's it for day one. Let's have a great year and learn something new every day."

As the students walk out, Mr. Watson stops Dex.

"Hey, it's Dexter, right? From what I remember in attendance."

Dex and Cain stop as they're both about to walk out of the classroom.

"Yeah, Mr. Watson, that's me, or you can call me Dex." Dex and Cain exchange a look, and Cain continues to walk out.

"Hey Cain, don't go too far. I'd like to speak with you after I talk with Dex."

At this point, both Cain and Dex think they're getting in trouble for talking and laughing during class. Mr. Watson closes the door, and Cain waits outside in the hall. In a soft tone, Mr. Watson says to Dex:

"Hey, that's your homeboy, right?"

Dex looks at Mr. Watson and lets out a confused chuckle at how Mr. Watson speaks when he isn't teaching.

"Um, yeah, he is. Why?"

"Oh, I just saw how close you guys seemed, and I noticed you pretty much talked him into sharing today. I was just thinking about having our first official lecture and lab based on sickle cell."

Dex raises his eyebrows, showing obvious interest.

"However, I didn't want it to come off disrespectful to him, so I wanted to ask both of you but start by asking you separately—to get your opinion."

Dex, excited, grabs the door and calls for Cain to come back in.

"Dex, wait..." Mr. Watson wasn't quite ready to ask Cain.

Cain walks in, and Dex closes the door.

"I brought up the idea to teach here about him teaching the class..."

Clark clears his throat, interrupting Dex. "Mr. Watson, that is."

"Yeah, sorry. Mr. Watson says he'd be able to teach the class about sickle cell if you're okay with it."

Cain is confused and doesn't know what to say. The silence is broken by Mr. Watson.

"Cain, I know it sounds crazy to you, but I believe it would work out fine. Listen, besides being a teacher and having my PhD, I specialize in sickle cell anemia. So, hearing that my student is a warrior, I wanted to reach out and see if you'd be okay with the first lecture being sickle cell-related?"

Cain looks at Dex, and Dex looks at Mr. Watson.

"So, this wasn't actually your idea, Dex?"

"Well, no, but I knew you'd be more open to it if I brought it up. But it's true, I did agree and wouldn't mind learning more."

Cain looks at the teacher. "What's in it for me? A lesson on my problems? To let my peers know my business? To use me as the lab rat or example? I appreciate the thought, but I'm out."

Cain leaves the classroom, leaving Dex and Mr. Watson standing there.

"Well, that went..."

"Perfect!" Dex cuts Mr. Watson off.

Mr. Watson looks at Dex with confusion. "Perfect?" he asks.

"Yes, perfect. You don't know Cain like I do. Go ahead and prepare your lecture and whatever labs you have for the week on sickle cell, and I'll talk to Cain. Trust me!"

Dex walks out in an attempt to catch up with Cain. Suddenly, the teacher's door opens again, and Dex sticks his head back in, looking at Mr. Watson. "Oh yeah, this means double A's for me and Cain on this week's assignment, by the way."

The door shuts, leaving Mr. Watson laughing at his desk. "It's going to be a long semester with that one," he says, referring to Dex.

Chapter 13

<u>Behind Closed Doors</u>

With a full day of classes now coming to an end it seems everyone has an important task to get things prepared. Also seems that all tasks lead back to Cain aka patient Sickled Shock. Definitely going to be an interesting week in the city of Portsville.

Classes at Portsville high fluctuate to every other day. So, Cain and Dex won't have science or any of the same classes from Monday. They won't have any of those classes until Wednesday. This now gives time not only for Dex to convince Cain, but also for Mr. Watson to get his lecture planned out and ready to teach the class.

The next morning at the bus stop Dex and Cain still go through the normal routine despite the little disagreement at science class yesterday. Cain goes to dap up Dex.

"Wassup bro?"

"Nothing much Cain, wassup with you. Didn't see you much at school yesterday after science class. You all good?"

Not knowing how Cain would respond he barely looks at Cain.

"I'm good, a little bit after lunch, like in between lunch and third block I started having a minor sickle cell crisis, but I'm all good."

Dex quickly snaps his head at Cain. "Oh shoot, my bad bro I hope it wasn't too bad, I'm glad to see you made it to the stop today then."

"Yeah, you know I'll be good though don't worry about me. Also sorry about the little outburst I had yesterday after class."

Dex daps up Cain again to reassure him he didn't take it the wrong way at all. "It's all-good man you know we are cool. Nothing like that would ever change things."

Cain goes through with the dap but still goes on to plead his case. "Nah bro it wasn't right. You are just looking out for me and my health. It was just *first day back you know, Tony and Breezy still had me pissed off and I didn't wanna feel like a lab rat you know?"*

"I understand where you are coming from. My bad for even being down with that and agreeing with the teacher. I couldn't imagine how things are mentally with all that going on."

"Like I said though I'm not mad at you. Just a bad timing I feel like. It could be a good idea though. I thought more on it last night and I will be down for it. Honestly, it'll help get my story out there, maybe people will stop asking me why I'm so skinny or why my eyes are yellow. So, let's do it. I will swing by Mr. Watsons class today and let him know."

Dex looks at Cain with a look on his face just standing in silence. Cain looks at Dex after no response. "What did you do?" Cain asked Dex.

"Huh? Nothing, I didn—"

"I know you too well Dex. What did you do?" as he cuts Dex off.

"Weelll... I might have told teach to go on with the lecture and I would talk to you about it."

Cain punches Dex in the arm.

"Oww, okay that was deserved, but you might regret it." As Dex rubs his arm and smiles.

"Now what Dex?"

"We will both get A's on this week's assignments and labs."

As the bus pulls up to the stop Cain puts his arm around Dex putting him in a playful headlock as they both laugh and walk on to the bus.

"You're stupid you know that right?" Cain says while laughing.

As for Mr. Watson, with classes being held every other day, he doesn't have to be at the school until later in the evening. Mr. Watson or Clark, rather, takes that time to do what Dex told him. He fully puts his trust in his student and goes on to get his lecture situated as well as plan for the lab. All in hopes that Dex can convince Cain to go on with the lecture on sickle cell. When it comes to the lecture it's easy for him to start considering he is a sickle cell specialist, he knows how to go with the flow and speak on the disease freely.

He is more concerned about just jumping into a lab not quite knowing what to do. Since Clark is still in the Doctor field, he takes a visit to the hospital to get some inspiration. To start Clark walks to the employee lab closet across from the blood bank. With him being a doctor and a teacher, he was given free will by upper management to get any supplies he needed for school labs. While in the utility closet he grabs the normal. The beacons, a few pipettes, and some extra test tubes not knowing everything that's available back at school. He finishes up grabbing all the little accessories for a lab and heads out of the closet. Closing and locking the door he suddenly hears a voice come from behind him.

"*Hey, is that the one and only Clark Watson? Should I call you Doc. Or Mr. Watson right now?*"

Clark turns around laughing at the joke to shake it off. "*Ahh funny guy. I knew it was you Bloodworth. How you been?*"

Bloodworth starts laughing as well. "*Good, good. Just finished up my shift over here you know.*" As he points towards the blood bank door.

"*Gotcha, long day today or not really?*"

"*Not too bad today. I take it easy now a days though. So, what's up with you? Getting lab supplies for class I'm assuming?*"

"*Yeah, actually I am. Got a lab going on tomorrow actually.*"

A look of sudden shock just hit Clark as he just now remembered the true dark secrets behind Bloodworth and what he does.

He looks at Bloodworth and quietly says. "*Can we talk somewhere else?*"

Leaving Bloodworth confused he answers with. "*Yeah, let me hit the restroom quick and I will* meet you in the parking lot. You parked in the employee section, right?"

"Yeah, I did. Okay sounds good. See you then."

As Clark walks away, he says to himself I can't believe I forgot what Bloodworth is capable of and can't believe I'm just now thinking about using his things for my lab.

Sam Bloodworth, the incredible trustworthy, hardworking, honest, set to the books blood bank physician. Well, that's what Van and the rest of the medical team in the hospital think about Sam Bloodworth. Not everyone knows the deep dark secrets behind Bloodworth.

Let's just say the stunt he pulled with Van and stealing the blood vial wasn't his first rodeo. Bloodworth secretly takes all types of blood vials from random discards for research and learning about different diseases within the blood. He is essentially a dark scientist who goes past all legal rights for his own personal lab and experiments. All within the shadows and no one knowing besides Clark Watson and potentially others.

Once at the car Clark puts all the supplies, he gathered from the closet in his trunk and waits for Bloodworth to show. Time goes by and Bloodworth finally shows up.

"Hey Clark, you wanted to talk about something?"

Clark looks around as Bloodworth gets closer. He then looks at Bloodworth.

"*You still...?*" Stopping mid sentence and giving Bloodworth a head nod as if he is supposed to know what he is talking about.

"*Possibly?*" He hesitates to answer while scanning the parking lot. "*Why who's asking?*"

"*You don't have to worry about any of that. I'm asking. I need some blood samples or vials for my lab. I know it's hard to crack down on specifics but preferably a vial with sickle cell. As my lecture will be on the topic of sickle cell.*"

Bloodworth instantly thinks about patient Sickled Shock and the blood vial that he still has preserved within a high-tech chemical fridge that he built himself.

Managing to keep blood for more than 48 hours is already hard. Bloodworth is so dark with his experiments he has managed to come up with technology and chemicals to keep blood for 16 years plus.

"*Oh yeah, I have this one vial in mind that could be perfect for that. Quick question though Clark. Or Should I say Mr. Watson!?*"

"*Quit doing that. I let it go the first time, but what's the question?*" As Clark looks at him a little aggravated.

"No trace of this coming back to me for one. Also how will this be justified with you having possession of the blood though?"

"No one should question it, but also, I'm a science teacher as well as a doctor. Sounds pretty justified to me, no?"

"Fair point. Just follow me to my house then."

Bloodworth walks away towards his car and they both head out.

Just a little over 10 minutes of driving Bloodworth pulls into his driveway. Shortly after Clark pulls in behind him. Once inside the house Clark goes on to say. "Man, I haven't been over here in a while. Still looks the same too to be honest."

Bloodworth looks at Clark while locking the door behind them. "Yeah, well don't get too comfortable. In and out you here."

Bloodworth walks towards the door that would normally lead to the garage. However, Bloodworth had it rigged up to a keypad that opened a separate portion of the house. He looks at Clark before putting in the keycode.

"Turn the other way."

Clark turns around listening to the beeps of the keypad. The door opens and they both enter a science lab filled with every type of scientific equipment you could imagine. Bloodworth enters yet another code on this refrigerator-looking device. The device opens and breaks down into multiple sections. The device is filled with multiple vials of blood throughout the entire thing. Bloodworth pulls out the one labeled "0420BB1995"

He rips the label off before Clark could read it and slaps on a label that read "Intended for scientific use only". He hands the vial to Clark along with a handheld mini fridge device one could say.

"Here is the vial and store it in this to keep the temperatures right and keep it preserved."

Clark looks at the vial and back at Bloodworth. "Sooo you have these labels and questioned me about getting away with this?"

"Can never be too safe with this. Now go on about your day. Also remember, you saw nothing, and I have nothing to do with you receiving that blood."

Clark leaves the house and gets prepared for tomorrow's class.

Chapter 14

Shadows of the Storm

The city of Portsville woke up to a rather hazy morning this Wednesday. No one thought anything of it because of the random weather changes that often happen within Portsville. Little did they know this would be a day full of adventure. Cain and Dex are yet to realize the day they are about to go through is filled with more than just the typical high school drama. Cain was never the one to back down from any challenges, but even he could admit this day was not going to be easy with Mr. Watsons lecture hanging over his head.

Cain as always sends up a prayer for the day before he gets his day started. This time asking for strength and courage to get through his class today without stress and without anyone looking at him differently after learning about his sickle cell. Things already felt different as Cain and Dex didn't talk much today at the bus stop. It was the normal handshake, but the conversation didn't start this time until on the bus.

"Yo Cain you good bro? You seem a little out of it."

Cain looks at Dex and responds. *"Yeah, I'm good bro something about today just feels different for real though. Could just be about class today, but I'm not sure if it is. Everything seems off I just feel like something is going to happen today."*

Dex bumps Cain on the arm. *"I thought it was just me having that feeling honestly, but yeah could be this class with Mr. Watson today, but it'll all work out for the better trust me."*

"Yeah man I just hope I make it to class today. You already know Tony and Breezy are going to start with some nonsense this morning and truthfully, I'm not here for the games this early today."

Tensions seem high already. The air in the sky of Portsville seems a lot thicker today than any other day. Dex is now hoping he didn't make any mistakes by telling the teacher to continue with the lecture and hoping he didn't turn his friend against him in any way.

"*Don't worry about Breezy or Tony. As far as class goes, it will be way better than expected. Stop worrying about it all Cain. Just let it be what it is. I got your back.*"

The bus pulls up to the school and lets everyone out. Once in the halls Cain and Dex go to the normal meeting spot before class with all their friends. To no surprise, minutes later here comes Breezy and Tony walking in between the group of friends that were in a circle.

Breezy looks at Dex. "*Wassup Dex!*" Then looks over to Cain "*Cain!*"

Dex answers back leaving Cain who didn't speak or acknowledge Breezy. Breezy turns and looks at Tony. Tony shrugs and says to Cain and Dex.

"*Wassup punks!*"

It takes Dex to speak up knowing Cain isn't having the best of days. "*Look we not really feeling this today if you two could just move on.*"

Breezy walks closer to Cain as Tony follows up stepping closer to Dex. Tony says. "*I don't remember you calling the shots around here.*"

While Breezy is looking at Cain he says. "*Well, what's wrong with you Mr. Alien?*" Referring to Cains jaundiced eyes.

"I know you heard us speaking." Breezy laughs and looks back at Tony. "Look at his yellow eyes Tony. He has to be an Alien or something."

The two start laughing as they don't realize what may be jokes to them is hurtful towards Cain as he can't help that his eyes are yellow.

Cain finally had enough and spoke out while slightly backing Breezy out of his face. "Wassup Breezy and Tony. I'm not feeling this today like Dex said. So, if the two of you could just leave us alone and go on about your day today."

Breezy looks down at Cains arm on his chest as he is being slightly pushed back. "Did you just touch me?"

Cain looks at Dex as he knows Breezy isn't going to let up. While staring down Cain Breezy goes on to ask. "Ay Tony, did he just touch me?"

Breezy goes to grab Cain by the collar of his shirt while saying. "Don't you ever put your han... ooff."

Cain pushes Breezy off him with way more force this time making Breezy stumble over somebody's foot and falling to the ground. Tony stands there in shock as Dex grabs Cain not knowing what will happen next. Breezy gets up quicker than he fell and chargers after Cain.

Beeeeeep! The bell rings for class.

Tony grabs Breezy to calm him down as a teacher walks by. *"Get to class fellas I know you heard the bell!"* The teacher says while walking down the hall.

Once again Tony and Breezy getting by without getting in trouble. Everyone calms down and Breezy says to Cain as they all walk in separate directions. *"You will regret that just you wait!"*

Once in class Cain and Dex sit down in the back of the class again. The words "**SICKLE CELL**" written in bold capital letters across the whiteboard. Dex ignored the whiteboard excited about what just went down in the hallway.

"Cain bro you good? Yo I've never seen you in that mode before. That was intense." Dex says in excitement laughing at the situation making Cain smirk.

"Yeah bro I'm good like I said on the bus I'm just tired of those two really thinking they can run everybody. Might not be me, but someone is really going to hurt them one day for that bully stuff man." Cain responded all while staring at the whiteboard.

Dex continues on ignoring the whiteboard still. *"Did you see his face after he hit the ground?"* Dex burst out laughing. *"He was so confused."*

Cain lets out a chuckle and follows up with *"You're dumb bro. Look at the board though."*

"Oh." Dex says instantly snapping out of the laugh. "*I guess teach was serious, but hey bro trust this will be good.*"

Cain shrugs. "*We will see.*"

Beeeeeep! The final bell rings, and Mr. Watson walks in.

"*Hello, class, good morning. Hope all is well with everyone today. I'm sure from the board, you all know what today's class will be about.*"

Cain and Dex notice that Mr. Watson is carrying a small gadget they've never seen before, as well as a new device sitting on the front desk. Cain looks at Dex, who is more familiar with technology.

"*Do you know what any of those are?*" Cain asks Dex.

"*The one in his hand? No, that's unfamiliar to me. It looks homemade, honestly. The one on the desk looks like some sort of electrical impedance device. Not sure if that's what it is, though.*"

Mr. Watson begins his lecture. "*As you know, from last class, we shared stories about our health. One student seemed to capture everyone's attention. I took it upon myself, with approval from that student, to have a lecture on what was discussed on Monday.*"

Cain leans over to Dex. "*At least he didn't name-drop. That makes me feel a bit better. It's* not all about me now. More of an actual class, in a way."

Dex nods in agreement.

"Now, this device in my hand is simply to hold this vial of blood I have for science purposes. Which brings me to my next point: because we'll be working with actual blood, some of you didn't have the lab safety release form signed yet. Therefore, the following students will not be able to participate in the hands-on portion of the lab." Mr. Watson names a few of the students without the signed permission form.

"The device here on the desk is an electrical impedance device for sickle cell detection within a blood sample."

Dex looks at Cain and smiles, feeling good about being right about the device. Mr. Watson continues with his lecture, informing the class that he is a sickle cell specialist, and encourages students to ask questions throughout. Mr. Watson starts with the basics of sickle cell, explaining how it affects red blood cells and changes their shape. He explains how blockage of cells causes pain throughout the body, leading to many complications, including fatigue. Mr. Watson also highlights the importance of understanding how sickle cell affects, but is not limited to, people of

African, Mediterranean, and Middle Eastern descent. He then moves on to discuss jaundice.

"Because sickle cell red blood cells die off more quickly than normal, the body is forced to process more hemoglobin, overwhelming the liver. This leads to the build-up of bilirubin, which causes the yellowish color in the eyes of those affected."

Dex looks at Cain. *"Yo, bro, I'm really learning a lot. Now I understand the jaundice thing and why you snapped on Breezy like you did."*

Cain looks at Dex and shakes his head while laughing because Dex keeps bringing up the hallway situation again.

Mr. Watson's lecture goes on for about another 30 minutes. He's forced to stop mid-sentence after hearing thunder in the distance.

"Well class, if there are no questions, I say we jump into the lab before that random storm in the distance gets closer. Since we are working with electricity today, let's have Cain or Dex go first, followed by everyone else."

Cain looks at Dex and gives him a slight head nod. *"You first, bro. I live this life! I know how things look."*

Dex walks up to the front, followed by Cain and the rest of the class, who huddle around. Mr. Watson puts on gloves, safety glasses, and an apron, then proceeds to hand out the same equipment to the students who are allowed to participate. While the class puts on their equipment, Mr. Watson takes the blood vial out of the handheld device, and the students watch in awe. He then places a sample of the blood on the electrical device and the microscope next to it. With the thunder seemingly getting closer, Mr. Watson quickly explains how the device works.

"This device uses an electrical current to detect sickle-shaped cells within the blood sample. Because these cells have different shapes than normal red blood cells, the device should detect any sickled red blood cells. Then we can move on to the microscope to view them."

After Dex uses the electrical device, he moves to the microscope to view the red blood cells. In between the switch, he looks at Cain and says, *"I know it' might be a different story for you, but this is really cool to learn about and see, Cain."*

Cain uses the impedance detection device, but things take a turn for the worse. As Cain continues to work with the device, a loud boom shakes the building from the nearby thunderstorm. Suddenly, another thunderous boom follows, knocking out the lights and causing an electrical surge similar to the one that happened when Cain was born. This surge travels through the electrical device Cain was using, causing it to explode and send an electrical shock through his body, knocking him to the back of the classroom. The class, including Mr. Watson and Dex, goes into a complete panic.

"CAIN!"

The power flickers from the surge and then comes back on. Mr. Watson and Dex are the first to rush to the back of the classroom to check on Cain.

"Don't touch him!" Mr. Watson says. "He could still be carrying a current through his body. Dex, go grab the broom and unscrew the wooden stick so we can at least make sure he's responsive. You call 911!" As he points to another student.

The student calls 911, and Dex rushes to get the broom. Meanwhile, Mr. Watson continues to attempt to talk to Cain, who lies on the floor, propped up by the wall.

"Cain! Cain, are you alright? Cain, can you hear me? Cain!"

With no one else around but Mr. Watson, Cain slightly opens his eyes, revealing the same static shock within his pupils that nurse Van saw at his birth. He only opens his eyes briefly, making Mr. Watson assume it was the electrical charge still coursing through Cain's body.

Dex returns with the broomstick, gently tapping and pushing on Cain's leg, getting no response. "*Cain, bro, can you hear me? Please. Cain!*"

Moments pass, and the first responders arrive, taking precautions to ensure Cain isn't still carrying any electrical charge within his body. They take him to the hospital, leaving the class and Dex in disbelief over what had just happened.

Mr. Watson unplugs all the equipment and continues packing everything up. As he places the device with the vial in his bag, he notices that the vial is now glowing. Mr. Watson quickly packs everything into his bag, confused by what's going on.

"*Class, I'm sorry things went so unexpectedly with that lab. I guess something happened with the weather, and the current the device was pulling caused a surge that unfortunately hit Cain hard. Let's just keep Cain in our prayers. Dex! Are you okay?*"

Dex sits in silence.

– Van ended up being right, after all. It all came full circle, but it only took 16 years. Also, where did that storm go? The mysterious thunderstorm disappeared after everything that happened. –

Chapter 15

Lightning in the Veins

Not quite the hospital visit Cain expected. Sickle cell is usually the cause of a hospital trip, but this time, it's something different. After school let out, a little after classes ended, Mr. Watson arrived at the hospital to check on Cain. When he entered, he saw Dex sitting in the waiting room with Cain's parents. Mr. Watson approached Dex and the family.

"Hey, Dex, how are you?"

"Hey, Teach, I'm good. Just waiting on things, you know. Oh, this is Cain's mom and dad."

Mr. Watson extended his hand to greet the family.

"Hello, Loranes, right? I'm Clark Watson, your son's teacher. I'm so sorry about what happened earlier today. I hope everything is working out and that he fully recovers. I feel terrible for all of this."

Cain's father reached out to shake Clark's hand. "Hey, Mr. Watson."

Clark cut him off. "Please, call me Clark."

"Well, Clark, we appreciate you. Dex told us everything. Don't worry about what happened—it was just a freak accident. We really appreciate you taking the time to teach the class about sickle cell. That was amazing. Thank you."

"Of course, it's no problem at all. How's Cain?" Cain's father looked over at Cain's mother before sitting back down. "I'll let her explain. She's better at remembering everything the doctor says."

Cain's mother looked up at Clark. Her eyes were red and swollen from crying. "Um, yeah, he's good. Just a lot of recovery ahead. He has a concussion from hitting the floor or wall, I think. He's stable, though. They won't let anyone back just yet. We're just hoping this doesn't trigger a sickle cell crisis. Right now, they're telling us he's resting."

She reached out to shake Clark's hand. "*Like my husband said, thank you again for everything. Dex says you're a great teacher. We really appreciate you. Please, sit with us.*"

"*Oh, thank you. I'm going to the restroom first. I just wanted to check on you guys and Cain first. Do you need anything?*"

Everyone responded with a polite "*No, thank you.*"

Clark excused himself and walked away to the restroom. As he walked through the hallway, he bumped into Bloodworth.

"*Well, well, well, look who it is. Mr. Dr. Watson.*"

Clark gave Bloodworth a look of distaste. "*Hey, Clark. Didn't mean to piss you off. What are you doing here?*"

"*It's a lot going on right now. Just came to check on my student after that tragic lab incident. That's all.*"

Bloodworth instantly panicked and pulled Clark into the bathroom. He looked around to make sure no one else was inside any of the stalls, then turned to Clark. "*Did—*"

Clark cut him off. "*Relax, you've got nothing to worry about. It was just a simple mishap with the weather and the equipment we were using.*"

Bloodworth paused, confused. "*Weather?*"

"Yeah, that thunderstorm that came by."

"Clark, I've been here since 7 AM, and it's almost 6 PM. There hasn't been any thunder at all today!"

Clark stood there, stunned, trying to process what Bloodworth had just said. He left Bloodworth standing in the doorway and continued to the stall using the restroom. He walks over to the sink washing his hands and goes on to splash his face with water. Finally, he spoke. "No thunder at all?"

"I haven't heard a peep of it all day," Bloodworth replied.

Clark was now truly confused. How could the storm he had heard earlier be non-existent? Especially with the school and hospital being so close to each other. The more he thought about it, the more it felt like something was off.

Bloodworth looked at Clark, then asked with concern, "What exactly happened in the lab?"

Clark started to explain the whole situation, and as he leaned in to whisper, he said, "I think I saw a static charge in Cain's eyes after everything went down."

Bloodworth tried to remain calm, but his disbelief was apparent. "Static charge in his eyes? Come on, Clark. That sounds like something out of a comic book. The electrical shock is fine, but the glowing vial and the static in the kid's eyes? You need some rest, man."

Clark shrugged, determined. "Say what you want. I know what I saw."

Walking out of the bathroom, they were met by Dex, who had just entered.

"Hey, Teach, isn't it weird how the thunder just stopped after all of that happened? That's crazy, right? What are the chances?"

Dex didn't wait for a response, just walked right past them and into the bathroom, leaving Clark and Bloodworth in shock. Clark looked at Bloodworth with a knowing glance before walking away, as if to say, "I told you so."

Bloodworth stood there, completely confused, unsure of what to make of all this. He slowly starts putting two and two together now hearing about the eyes of the student and connecting it to the story Van told him about the baby eyes 16 years ago.

Clark went back to the waiting room to sit with Cain's family until they received more news. Meanwhile, Bloodworth sprinted up to the blood bank floor. He walked in and told his coworker that he had just gotten sick in the bathroom and needed her to finish the last hour alone until the shift change at 7. As upper management, she didn't question it. Bloodworth clocked out and rushed to his car to make a phone call.

Doo-Doo-Doo

The call ended instantly.

Bloodworth didn't give up. He quickly dialed the number again thinking it was on do not disturb

This time, he got a different sound.

Beep.

The call went through.

Riiing... Riiing.

Vrrr-Vrrr-Vrrr. The phone vibrated on the other end.

Click!

A long pause followed, then a voice answered groggily, as if they had just woken up. *"Hello?"*

Another long pause.

Finally, Bloodworth spoke.

"Van! Patient Sickled Shock... yeah, he is alive!"

Chapter 16

The Weight of the Past

Van sits up in bed, places the phone down on her lap, and rubs her eyes. She glances over at the clock and sees it's 6:05 p.m. She picks the phone back up, sitting still as she tries to figure out if she was dreaming or not.

"*Hello?*" Van says again, still confused.

"*Hey, Van! It's me, Bloodworth. Not sure if you heard me, but patient Sickled Shock… He…*"

Van cuts him off. "*How do you know?*"

Bloodworth looks around the parking lot as he sits in his car, nervous about the story he just heard. "*I just got off work. I had to leave early, so*

I don't want to talk on the phone about it, nor do I want to talk while sitting in the parking lot. Sounds like I might have woken you up, so let's meet at my house in, like, 30-45 minutes?"

"Sounds good. I'll be there."

The phone call ends, and Van gets up to get dressed. *Well, so much for getting my rest and going to bed early today,* Van thinks to herself.

Back at the hospital, Cain has been moved to the ICU for added protection, as they need to monitor him closely since he's still not awake, though in stable condition. Only two visitors are allowed in at a time, so Dex and Clark wait in the lobby while the Loranes go back to see their son.

Dex, looking down and fidgeting with his hands, asking Mr. Watson without looking up, "Hey, teach... I'm sorry... Mr. Watson, do you think Cain will be alright? Do you think he'll pull through?"

Mr. Watson, watching Dex fidget, responds, "Of course, Dex. He's got this. If I know anything about a warrior... a sickle cell warrior, he will be just fine. Warriors of sickle cell are often built different. He'll be back better than ever."

Dex looks up at Mr. Watson. "Why did this happen, do you think? Also, why did that thunderstorm only last for, like, 30 minutes and stop right after the power surge? It almost feels like it was destined to happen."

"Yeah, it was strange. Not sure what that was about, to be honest. Let's just stay focused on being strong for Cain and his family. We'll work on what's next, you know?"

"Yeah, true!" Dex responds, sinking into his seat.

Mr. Watson looks at Dex. "By the way, it's okay to call me 'teach' now."

Dex looks up at Mr. Watson and smirks.

A little over 30 minutes later, Cain's mother and father come out of the room. Dex and Clark are still in the waiting room. Cain's father walks over to talk with them as his mother heads to the restroom.

"How is he?" Dex asks quickly, sitting up in his seat.

"He's good. Still waiting for him to wake up on his own, but the doctors are saying he'll make a full recovery. No brain damage, and he doesn't seem paralyzed. Of course, they'll have to check again once he wakes up. You two can go see him if you'd like."

Dex looks over at Mr. Watson. "I don't think I want to see him like this. I'll just wait for him to wake up."

Clark then responds, "Yeah, just out of respect, I don't want to go back either. I just wanted to wait and see how everything went tonight. Dex, did you want a ride home?"

"No thanks, I think I'll stay here a little longer."

"Okay, sounds good. If I don't see you in the halls tomorrow, hopefully I'll see you in class on Friday. Nice to meet you, sir." Mr. Watson leaves the hospital, leaving Dex and Cain's parents in the waiting room.

It's almost time for Van to pull up to Bloodworth's house. Once Van parks in the driveway and turns off the car, she lets out a huge exhale. At this point, she's mentally going through it, unsure whether to be excited or scared that this might cause more issues.

Before she can even knock on the door, it swings open, and Bloodworth walks away towards the living room with a notebook in his hand and a glass of brown liquid with ice, leaving the door open and Van standing outside. *How did he know I was here?* Van thinks to herself. She enters cautiously, closing the door behind her.

"Hey... um, Bloodworth, you okay?"

"Yeah, come in. I have to tell you what happened today." Bloodworth sits on the couch, taking a sip of his drink, while Van joins him shortly after.

Bloodworth takes another sip from his glass before beginning to tell the story that Clark shared with him in the bathroom.

"So, Clark Watson—the teacher, doctor—was in the hospital today..." He proceeds to tell the entire story of what happened. Once he finishes, Van immediately starts firing out questions.

"Why would you give out that vial? I thought you said you got rid of it? Are you talking about Clark Watson, the kid from 16 years ago who talked to us during the meeting? How is the student? Why would you use that vial? Are we sure this is Patient Sickled Shock? What thunderstorm? And Clark said something about the glowing vial and eyes first?" Van falls back, sinking into the couch, still processing everything.

"Well, I'm not going to answer all of those," Bloodworth says. "Yes, that's the Clark Watson from the meeting 16 years ago, and I honestly gave him a sample of the blood—not all of it. But that's beside the point. Patient Sickled Shock is out there, and that's what matters."

"So, what now?" Van responds with obvious aggravation after finding out about the vial.

"That's the next step—we have to figure that out."

"I truly just want to know he's safe and living a good life, and then I'll be happy with that."

Bloodworth looks at Van, as if that's not all he wants from this whole situation. He closes his notebook and just nods in agreement with Van's statement. But something about Bloodworth seems off—like he has something else planned.

Van, now on edge, speaks up, "Bloodworth, there's more to this, isn't there? Something you're not telling me—"

But before she can finish, he glances over his shoulder, his face tightening.

"Some things are better left untouched, Van."

Chapter 17

In the Wake of Shock

Thursday morning feels different at the bus stop. No Cain. As Dex heads to school, he knows he'll have to get through the day without running into Breezy and Tony. But, as usual, things don't go as planned. The moment Dex steps into the hall, he's met by Breezy and Tony. Luckily, the bus was a little later than usual, so the hallway chat won't be as long.

"*Well, well, so your friend decides to push me to the ground and not show up for school today, huh?*" Breezy says with a mocking tone.

"Hey Breezy, it's not even like that. Well, the push was, but he was in a freak accident in class yesterday. He's in..." Dex starts.

Tony cuts him off. "Let me guess, the hospital? It's always the same with that guy. It's getting old now."

Dex looks at Tony in disbelief.

Beeeeeep!

"Oh, it's getting old, right? Kinda like you two bullying the school? Right? Grow up." Dex walks away, heading to class, leaving Breezy and Tony standing there.

Vrrr. Vrrr. Vrrr.

Elaine picks up the phone. "Hello?"

"Hey, it's Van. Just wanted to call and keep in touch more often."

Elaine sits up on her couch and mutes her TV. "Oh, Van, hey! I'm happy to hear from you. How's everything been?"

The two chat, catching up on life, grandkids, gossip, and old times. They reminisce about their days working at the hospital together. Van talks about her cancer and life in general, and the conversation passes the hour mark. Eventually, Van brings up the topic of Patient Sickled Shock—aka Baby Cain, aka Cain Lorane.

"Hey, Elaine, do you remember the baby from like 16 years ago? The one I saw get shocked, and I was telling you about when we worked that one shift together?"

"Oh my gosh, yes! You were so in over your head—I couldn't calm you down for anything!" Elaine laughs.

"Well, yeah, you're right about that. But I don't think I was fully in over my head like you say. Besides having dreams about him on and off over these past 16 years, I've been trying to track him down to make sure he's been healthy and living a good life despite being shocked and having sickle cell."

Elaine pulls the phone away from her ear as if she's saying, Not this again. She realizes the conversation has been going on for over an hour. She puts the phone back to her ear just in time to hear Van say,

"And I've been working with Bloodworth to find the baby—well, now a teen. He might be alive and in the hospital right now."

Elaine pauses. The silence is heavy. "Hello, Elaine?" Van asks.

More silence.

"Did you say Bloodworth? As in Sam 'Dr. Vile' Bloodworth?"

Van pauses, startled. She knows both Bloodworth and Sam, but she's confused by Elaine's sudden mention of Dr. Vile. Finally, Van responds,

"Yeah, Sam Bloodworth. But who or what made you say Dr. Vile?"

Elaine skips over the question. "Hey, we really need to talk about this somewhere else and asap if this baby Cain situation is real."

Van looks around her house in a panicked shocked after finally hearing and remembering Cains' name over the years passed. She stands up while on the phone still, shouting at Elaine. "Cain! That's it! His name was Cain! How do you remember that?"

"Van! Now isn't the time! We seriously need to talk about this!" Elaine's voice becomes more urgent as she gets ready, shutting Vans' excitement off. "Van, I'm serious. Also, don't tell Bloodworth or talk to him at all within the next 15 minutes. I'm on my way over."

Silence fills the phone.

"Do you hear me?" Elaine asks.

"Yes, yes, okay, I hear you. I'll be here," Van says quickly.

Through the phone Van hears what seems to be a door slamming on Elaines end, followed by the click of the call ending. Van sits back down, her mind racing. She starts thinking about what just happened—how Elaine remembered Cain's name and why she's so determined to talk about Bloodworth or why she called Bloodworth Dr. Vial.

At the hospital, Cain still hasn't woken up after being shocked and knocked into a wall. He remains stable and breathing on his own, and could wake up at any moment. Since Cain was born, his hemoglobin was sitting at a normal sickle cell patient level of 6-7.5. However, after the school lab incident, his hemoglobin was tested and came back as high as 11.7. This is highly unusual for a sickle cell patient.

Cain's parents return from the cafeteria, where the doctors update them. No more breathing tubes—he's still stable—and the higher hemoglobin levels are likely due to the meds and breathing pumps they had Cain on to keep him stabilized. They mention that once he wakes up and is breathing more on his own, they'll recheck his hemoglobin to see if it drops back down.

Cain's mom goes back to the room while his dad works on a business call he had to attend. She sits by Cain's bed, talking to him, hoping that something will trigger him to wake up. As time goes by, she notices it's almost time for school to let out, so she starts talking about Dex and Mr. Watson, hoping that will wake Cain up. She mentions how all his friends at school probably miss him and hopes things aren't like freshman year without him.

After hours of random thoughts and out loud conversations with herself, Cain finally blinks and opens his eyes.

"Mm...Mom?"

She jumps out of her chair. "Oh, my baby! Yes, baby, I'm here. Are you okay?"

Cain slowly closes his eyes again.

"Cain, squeeze my hand, baby, if you can hear me."

Cain squeezes his mother's hand with an unexpected amount of pressure.

"Ohhh. Okay, okay, oww! Cain, I'll be right back—I have to get the nurse!"

She pulls her hand back, wincing from the pain, and runs out the door to get the nurses and Cain's father.

Chapter 18

Hidden Truths

Knock! Knock! Knock! The knocking sound is coming from outside of Vans house. Van gets up from her couch and goes over to open the door. *"Who is it?"*

Van asked while looking through the peep hole. *"It's me Elaine!"*

Van opens the door letting Elaine in and locking it behind her.

"Elaine how did you get here so quickly? It's usually like a 15-minute drive from your house, isn't it? You got here in less than 10 just about." Van

says as she chuckles not realizing how serious things are with Bloodworth.

Van goes on to being a proper host asking if Elaine wants anything to drink and telling Elaine to make herself comfortable.

"Yes, I will take a bottle of water if you have one, and I got here going 55 in a 40. I don't think you understand how serious this is with Bloodworth."

Elaine sits on the couch shaking her leg nervously. Van grabbed two bottles of water out of the fridge and walked over to Elaine, handing her a bottle of water and sitting down. Van notices her leg is shaking and looks at the intense worried face Elaine has.

"So, this is that serious? I'm not sure I know everything about Bloodworth. You're scaring me, Elaine."

Elaine takes a few big gulps of water and looks at Van. *"I need you to tell me every single thing that involves you and Sam. With as much detail as you can remember all the way back to the beginning from 16 years ago if you can."*

Van looks at Elaine with raised eyebrows and takes a deep breath and exhales.

"Okay get comfortable its quite a lot, but I will go through it quickly."

Van starts going over everything with Elaine starting back 16 years ago and how they stole the blood vial of baby Cain. As well as telling Elaine how the vial was found glowing by Bloodworth. From here she talks about how they just let time pass while keeping an eye/ear out for any potential signs of Cain over the years. She goes on about the dreams she's been having and states that she only wanted to know Cain was okay and living a good life. Van brings up how she was at Bloodworth's house recently and asked him what he did with the vial, and he blew her off not fully answering her. She goes on more about everything else she's done with Bloodworth up to now.

Elaine takes a sip of her water now. *"Wow, okay. Yeah. Let's just say Sam is not the guy you think. Not Everyone knows everything about him, so I don't blame you for not knowing."*

Van looks at Elaine with a look of interest noticing that Elaine doesn't call Bloodworth by anything other than his first name.

Elaine looks at Van. *"Listen I can't tell you how to go about it, but I would say don't do anything else with that guy. You got what you want and know Cain is alive now. If he tries to drag you down with him in any of this, I have your back. Sam Bloodworth is a terrible person. Some call him Dr. Vial. He has this thing where he takes vials of* blood from the blood bank and stores it in his secret scientist lab at his house."

Van is looking at Elaine now in shock. "Secret lab? But... But I've been to his house and saw nothing out of the ordinary."

Elaine sighs and shakes her head. "Of course not. He wants to use you as an escape if things go wrong and he gets caught he has you to blame. They call him Dr. Vial for a reason. An undercover blood bank physician using blood he takes for who knows what kind of research. We have to stop him now Van. I've always wanted to shut down his little operation. What a better time than now, with you. Plus who knows what he will do or could do with Cain now knowing he isn't quite the normal sickle cell warrior."

Van now at this point looks pissed off and no longer wants anything to do with Sam Bloodworth. She grabs both of Elaines hands and looks her in the eyes. "Please promise me that we will stick together through all of this, and I am sorry for keeping things from you and I hope we can stay friends and get back as close as we were 16 years ago. I'm sorry Elaine. That's the last thing I want is Cain to be hurt by Sam."

As Van refuses to use his last name anymore.

Elaine squeezes Vans hands. *"I promise Van! We will always be friends, and I refuse to let Dr. Vial do anything to you or Cain!"*

At the hospital now with Cain awake and his parents by his side things seem to be going well. Cain has been doing a lot better. Up actually eating now, and just about back to his normal self. Looking at an early discharge in the morning. Cains parents walk out as Dex walks in a little after.

"Yo Cain wassup bro? I've been checking on you like crazy. I'm glad you're better. Your mom told me you woke up, so I had to come see you."

Cain looks up with a smirk on his face happy to see Dex. *"Yo bro I'm good man thanks for checking I don't remember much of anything."*

"Yeah bro it was all crazy to me and the class. It was so sudden. We won't talk much about it now though bro." Dex says wanting Cain to rest more than talk.

Cain goes on missing the signs Dex is showing. *"So how have things been back at school with Breezy and Tony?"*

Dex shakes his head and walks closer to Cain. *"Man, they pushed up on me today actually. I had no choice but to stand up for myself and for you too honestly. I don't think things will be easy for us whenever we go back to school. I was lucky and saved by the bell today. Literally. Don't worry about those fools you gotta get your rest bro. They're the last thing you need to worry about."*

Cain shrugs. *"Yeah, I guess you're right we got this though bro. Imma be honest with you I feel a little stronger too. Definitely different than any other time spent in the hospital."*

"Probably because you got forced pushed into a wall because of electricity."

Dex chuckles, making Cain laugh a little. *"Shut up bro. you're so stupid."* As the two laugh.

Dex puts his hand on Cains shoulder. *"Hey bro listen..."*

A doctor, or what seems to be a doctor walks in the room. Dex stops talking, looks at the door, and back at Cain. *"Never mind we will talk later, get you some rest bro."*

Dex walks out leaving just Cain and the Doctor in the room.

"Hello, Cain right?"

Cain responds. *"Yessir that's me."*

While the doctor looks at Cain with an intense stare, he locks the door behind him and goes on to say. *"Good to know. My name is Dr. Vial."*

Chapter 19

Dr. Vial

Cain had been expecting the usual—a quick check-up, a few questions, maybe some jokes from Dex before he left. But this doctor, with his intense eyes and the way he locked the door behind him, told Cain it wasn't going to be the same. Something was off. Cain sat up in his bed, now nervous about what was happening.

Dr. Vial, also known as Sam Bloodworth to others, started walking closer to Cain. With each step, Cain's heart rate increased, his anxiety spiking. Dr. Vial placed his briefcase on a chair and then took out a blood vial and a needle.

"Now, Cain, this can all be nice and smooth. All I need is your blood, and then I'll give you some medicine through your IV so you won't remember any of this," Dr. Vial said, his voice smooth but chilling. "I believe you're different from anyone I've taken samples from."

Cain, now fully aware that this wasn't a regular doctor's visit, tensed. As Dr. Vial came closer to the bed, Cain balled his fists, preparing to fight back. His heart pounded, and he let out a scream for help.

"HELP!" Cain shouted, his voice loud and desperate.

When he opened his eyes, Dr. Vial was staring back at him, eyes locked on his. Dr. Vial saw a bolt of lightning flash through Cains pupils, repeatedly. The surge of energy that followed was uncontrollable. The TV in the room exploded from the electrical shock, and then Cain swung at the doctor, sending a shock pulse that pushed Dr. Vial all the way back to the door, causing him to crash to the floor.

Luckily for Dr. Vial, the strike wasn't as powerful as the one that hit Cain earlier. The doctor scrambled to collect his things, his expression filled with confusion and alarm, before quickly running out of the room.

Cain falls back in his bed, heavy breaths escaping him. The TV was smoking, and he was completely disoriented. He looked at his hands, flipping them over, inspecting his palms and the backs of his hands as they still looked normal.

Just five seconds after Dr. Vial ran out, a team of nurses rushed in, followed by Cain's parents.

"Cain, what happened? Are you alright?" his father asked, his voice full of concern.

"Yeah, I'm good. It's just this..." Cain paused, trying to make sense of what happened and realizing he should make up a lie about what just happened. "...It's just the TV exploded and woke me up."

One of the nurses started apologizing. "We're so sorry. We're not sure what happened, but the power flickered throughout the hospital, and the lights went out for a moment. Everything seems to be back to normal now."

Cain, still confused, looked around the room. "The lights in the hospital went out?"

"Yeah," his father confirmed. "There was a surge, or something. All the electronics and lights went out."

"Well, I'm just glad you're okay, baby," his mom said, her voice filled with relief. "So when will we move rooms?"

"We'll move him down the hall right now," the nurse replied.

His parents gathered Cain's belongings, and the nurses began pushing him down the hall. As they made their way, Dex emerged from the bathroom, rushing toward the stretcher.

"Cain, you good? What's going on? Are they taking you somewhere else?" Dex asked, looking worried.

"I'm good, bro. They're just moving me down the hall. Something happened in that room," Cain replied, his voice calmer than he felt.

Dex followed the stretcher, continuing to ask questions. "So, what did—"

Cain cut him off, sensing his friend didn't need the details right now. "The TV exploded. I'm good, though, bro."

Dex, understanding that it was a subject Cain didn't want to dive into, gave him a quick nod. "Okay, glad you're well, bro. I'll see you later."

Once in the new room, the nurse explained the plans for the night. "It looks like you've been improving over the last few hours. The doctors gave us the go-ahead to start the discharge paperwork and get you out of here early in the morning, if that's okay with you and if you're feeling up to it."

Cain glanced at his parents and then back at the nurse. "Yeah, I feel good. Honestly, I feel better than I've ever felt before."

"Great! I'll start the paperwork now, and we'll keep an eye on you through the night. Hopefully, you'll be out of here in the morning."

"Sounds good. I'm ready to get out of here—not trying to stay in the hospital any longer than I have to, especially for something other than sickle cell."

"Understandable. Let us know if you need anything."

"No, thank you."

"Mom, Dad, do you need anything?" the nurse asked as she prepared to leave.

"No, I think we're good," his mom answered, while his dad nodded.

The nurse left the room, and Cain looked over at his parents. He lay back in bed, staring at the ceiling lights, his mind racing with what had just happened.

"Hey, are you guys staying in here tonight?" Cain asked quietly, his voice uncertain.

"We always stay, Cain. What do you mean?" his mom replied, giving him a reassuring smile.

"No, I mean in here," Cain clarified. "This room seems a little bigger. You guys could stay in here instead of the lobby, right?"

"If that's what you want, I can stay in here with you tonight," his mom said, her voice soft.

"Dad can stay too. I just don't feel comfortable here right now. There's so much going on. Just spend time with me tonight, as a family," Cain urged.

His parents agreed, and they settled in, staying with Cain in the room. He fell asleep peacefully through the night, comforted by their presence, but still uneasy, not knowing if Dr. Vial might come back or not.

Chapter 20

Thunderous Blood

It was around 6 a.m. when the Lorane family was woken by soft knocks on the door. It was the same nurse from last night.

"Hey, Cain, how'd you sleep last night? And how are you feeling?" The nurse whispered, knowing it was early.

"I'm feeling pretty good. Slept as well as I could in a hospital, you know," Cain smiled.

"Well, we kept an eye on you last night, and everything seems to be back to normal. No concerns. I'm here to unhook you, remove your IV, and discharge you," she said.

"How's his hemoglobin now?" Cain's dad asked.

"It's surprisingly at an 11 still. It dropped a little, but it's still higher than usual, which is actually a good thing."

"Okay, great," his dad nodded.

The nurse began to remove Cain's IV and all the heart and oxygen equipment. As she did, a quick spark flared from the vein when the IV tube was removed. Cain was the only one to notice it. He glanced at the nurse, but she wasn't paying attention, focused on finding gauze to wrap up his arm. Cain felt a deep confusion—what was going on with his body? Why did Dr. Vial come to see him? And how had he caused the TV to explode?

On the way out of the hospital, Cain glanced at the time: it was only 6:15 a.m. He got into his parents' car and decided to ask, "Hey, can we stop to get food, and then you guys drop me off at school before it starts?"

Momma Lorane exchanged a look with Cain's dad before he shrugged. "You just got out of the hospital, baby. Are you sure you feel like going to school today?"

"Yeah, I feel great. Honestly, I don't feel like I've just been discharged from a sickle cell crisis. I'm not sore, I'm not tired, and I actually feel hungry this time." Cain smiled, trying to stay optimistic.

His dad grinned. *"Sounds good. What do you want to eat?"*

His mom nudged his dad with her elbow, clearly not convinced. *"Just don't overdo it, okay? Call us if you start feeling bad."*

They went to a local diner for breakfast. Cain ordered nearly everything except eggs: two strips of crispy bacon, two sausage links, hashbrowns, two pancakes, and cheese grits. His parents exchanged worried looks, considering how Cain wasn't usually a big eater, especially not for breakfast.

"Cain, are you sure you want all of that?" his dad asked.

"Yeah, I'm really hungry today. I'll eat it," Cain reassured him.

Still doubtful, his parents placed their orders. Once the food arrived, Cain dug in. He started with the grits, then moved on to the rest of his meal, finishing it all before his parents had even made a dent in theirs. He washed it down with orange juice and sat back, waiting for his parents to finish.

"Oh, wow, Cain, you were hungry, huh?" his mother said, surprised.

"Yeah, I feel different today. Maybe it was a good thing the lab test went wrong," Cain tried to stay positive, though he still couldn't shake his worry about Dr. Vial and the strange electricity inside him.

After breakfast, Cain realized it was still early enough for him to catch the bus instead of going straight to school.

"Hey, Dad, can you drop me off at the bus stop? I'll ride the bus with Dex since we still have time."

His dad agreed with the time they still had left and went on towards the neighborhood and bus stop. They arrived just as Dex showed up.

"CAIN!" Dex jogged over, grinning.

"Yo, what's up, Dex?" Cain said, dapping him up.

"Bro, you're the last person I expected to see today, especially after seeing you in the hospital last night."

"Yeah, man, it's been a lot going on. I gotta tell you what happened last night! Also, I want to know exactly what happened to me in the lab the other day."

Dex shook his head in disbelief. "Yeah, we definitely have a lot to talk about. I honestly don't even know how you're standing here talking to me right now." He gave Cain a hug, grateful his best friend was okay.

As they waited for the bus, Cain started explaining what happened the night before. "Bro, last night, that doctor who came in wasn't normal. Things went crazy after you left. He locked the door and told me his name was Dr. Vial. He pulled out a needle and started walking towards me. All I remember is screaming for help, and then the TV exploded with electricity. I swung at him, and a bolt of lightning shot out from my hand, hitting him and knocking him against the wall. He scrambled to grab his things and ran out before my parents and the nurses showed up."

Dex laughed at first, but when he saw Cain's serious face, he immediately stopped. "*Wait, you're serious? You're saying you have some sort of powers now?*"

Cain nodded firmly. "*Yeah, it sounds insane, I know, but I'm telling you, something's happening to me, Dex. Also, when the nurse took my IV out this morning, I saw a spark come from my arm.*"

Dex tried to stifle another laugh but managed to keep his cool. "*Well, if you're becoming a superhero, can I be your sidekick or your tech guy?*"

Cain rolled his eyes but smiled. "*Yeah, sure. But seriously, we need to figure this out. We need to keep it between us, though. This isn't just some random thing—it could be life or death. I'm not just fighting sickle cell anymore. I feel like Dr. Vial's not done with me yet. He knows more than we do, and I don't like it.*"

Dex's expression softened, and he sighed deeply. *"I got your back, Cain. We'll figure this out, no matter what."*

The bus pulled up to the school, and Dex and Cain headed to their usual meeting spot.

"Hey, Cain," Dex said thoughtfully, *"You think we should tell Teach? He's got a PhD and knows a lot about sickle cell. We might need him in the future."*

"You might be right, but I don't think this is sickle cell related at all," Cain replied. *"Let's just keep it low for now and see how things play out."*

"Bet!" Dex agreed.

As they walked down the hall, Cain gave Dex a playful push. Dex, startled, was sent flying into the lockers.

"Cain, bro, why'd you push me so hard?" Dex laughed, shaking his head.

"I swear, I didn't mean to push you that hard. My bad, bro." Cain's eyes widened in surprise. *"I'm telling you, something's different about me. I don't get it."*

Dex laughed it off. *"It's all good, I'm not mad."*

They continued down the hall toward their usual spot, where they found Breezy and Tony already waiting.

"Ohhh, look who it is," Breezy said finishing with. *"Mr. Push-People-and-Disappear."*

"Breezy, come on, dude, I pushed you because you were in my face after I told you I wasn't feeling it," Cain replied, trying to stay calm.

Tony smirked. "Hey Breezy, looks like someone forgot who runs these hallways. Show him what's up."

Dex stepped in before things escalated. "Listen, don't start today. Do you really have no feelings for someone who just got out of the hospital?"

"Ahh, be quiet, Dexter! Go find a computer to hide behind. My problem right now is with Cain, not you."

"Show him what's up, Breezy," Tony urged again.

Breezy threw a punch at Cain. As the punch came toward him, Dex noticed Cain's eyes flashing with electricity. The lights above them flickered and blew out. Cain, in an instinctive move, countered with a punch to Breezy's stomach, sending a bolt of electrical energy into him and knocking him back.

As Breezy stumbled back, the shock still running through him, he hit the ground hard, groaning in pain. The hallway was quiet, with only Dex and Tony staring at Cain in shock. Cain stood frozen, unsure of what had just happened. Breezy struggled to push himself up off the ground. Cain could feel his heart racing, still processing the power he hadn't meant to use. He glanced over at Dex, who was wide-eyed in disbelief. Whatever this was, it wasn't just some weird fluke—it was something far bigger than either of them had imagined.

Chapter 21

Tensions Rise

Sam Bloodworth, or Dr. Vial, sat in his home, his mind racing with confusion. He couldn't stop thinking about what he'd just witnessed. Not only had the TV exploded, but he'd been sent flying back by an electrical shock. It was more than a science experiment on a sickle cell patient—it was a revelation. This was no ordinary teenager. Cain had powers, and Bloodworth realized that this could be the patient he had been searching for all his life. This could be his ticket to wealth and power, but at what cost?

Bloodworth jotted down everything that had happened that night, already planning his next move: get a blood sample from Cain, and maybe even figure out a way to strip him of his newfound abilities.

Bloodworth had started his operation with hopes of curing diseases, but as the years went on, his obsession twisted into something darker. He'd gone from researching cures to taking blood samples from willing donors—then from the blood banks. His experiments grew more reckless as he sought a way to profit from his discoveries. Cain was the first patient he'd attempted to take blood from in person, hoping to use the samples for his experiments. But the results had been catastrophic, leaving a trail of untraceable deaths in the hospital. Nobody had suspected him, but that didn't matter anymore. Bloodworth was ready to cross every line for his ambition.

Losing his mother to blood cancer had driven him down this path. The obsession with understanding why she died—and with exacting revenge on the world for it—had warped his mind over time. His desire for vengeance turned into a ruthless ambition to take control of the fate of others.

Now, Cain was his golden ticket. Bloodworth knew that if he could harness Cain's abilities, he would have the power, fame, and fortune he craved. No one would stop him—not even the hospital staff, not even his conscience.

As Bloodworth plotted his next move, far away, Elaine and Van were preparing their own plans. Elaine had returned to Van's house, worried about how far Sam might go to get to Cain. Her fears weren't just for Cain; she was concerned about what Bloodworth might do to Van—and about Vans health.

"Hey Van, how have you been the past couple of days?" Elaine asked, trying to ease the tension.

Van, distracted and still not fully recovered from the side effects of her medication, sighed. "I've been okay. This medicine's making me a little sick, but I'm more worried about this Sam situation. Hopefully, he isn't as crazy as you say."

Elaine looked at her seriously. "Unfortunately, he is. Sam Bloodworth isn't sane, Van. I know enough about him to say that you're in more danger than you realize." She paused, trying to hide her exhaustion. "But don't worry. I'll shut him down myself if I have to. If you want out of this, I'll understand, but I'm in it to the end. Your health is more important."

Van looked at Elaine as if she were insane. *"Are you crazy? I brought you into this. No way am I leaving you to handle this alone."*

Elaine smiled at her resolve but could see the worry behind her eyes. *"So, you've been to Sam's house before, right? Have you noticed anything weird?"*

"Not really," Van replied, rubbing her temples. *"Nothing out of the ordinary."*

Elaine, now yawning, leaned forward. *"I doubt it's right out in the open. A scientist like Sam wouldn't just leave his operation sitting around for everyone to see. It has to be hidden—like a secret lab or something."*

Van hesitated, clearly uneasy. *"You're starting to scare me, you know that? Plus, you seem really tired. Are you letting this whole thing keep you up?"*

Elaine sighed. *"Yeah, I've barely slept since you told me about that vial of blood you took. Got any coffee?"*

Van didn't respond immediately, but after a long pause, she just sat there, lost in thought. Elaine, taking the initiative, went to the kitchen to brew the coffee herself.

Once she returned, coffee in hand, she plopped down beside Van and took a sip. *"So, how about we* sneak into Sam's house tonight and see what we can find?"

Van jumped back in shock. *"Are you insane?"*

Elaine blinked in surprise. *"What? I asked if you had coffee. You didn't say anything. I'm sorry, I'll buy you more if that's what's bothering you."*

Van threw her hands up in frustration. *"Forget the coffee! What do you mean 'sneak into Sam's house'? You can't be serious."*

Elaine smirked. *"Well, unless you have a better idea for how to stop him. I'm all ears."*

Van fell silent, the weight of the situation sinking in. She couldn't just leave things to chance, but neither could she ignore her own health—or the danger they were in.

Then it hit her. *"Wait. Remember how Sam said that Clark Watson asked him for blood samples? What if we find Clark first?"*

Elaine's eyes lit up. *"Mmm, and then we all sneak into Sam's house. That could work!"*

Van wasn't sure she wanted to be part of a 'sneak into Sam's house' plan, her idea made a little more sense. *"Let's try finding Clark later, but we haven't seen him in sixteen years. Who knows how he looks now?"*

Beeeeeep! The first school bell rang.

Meanwhile, Dex and Tony stood frozen in shock as Breezy layed on the ground. Cain, still looking at his hands in disbelief, was trying to process everything that had just happened. Tony quickly ran over to Breezy, pulling him up and rushing off to class. With the bell going off no one really noticed the situation between Breezy and Cain besides Tony and Dex.

"Let's go, dude. I always knew something was up with Cain, but not like this," Tony muttered as they hurried away.

Tony and Breezy both run away to class, potentially being the last time, they ever bully someone within the halls of Portsville high. Dex and Cain walked toward their class, neither saying much. They sat down at the back, and after a moment, Dex spoke.

"What was that, bro? Not saying I didn't believe you before, but now... I get it."

Cain stayed silent, still processing his own thoughts. Dex nudged him again. "Bro, are you like a superhero now or something?"

Cain shot him a glance with a worried face. "I don't know, man," he shrugged. "I think I'm just figuring it out as I go."

Beeeeeep! The final bell rang, signaling the start of class, and Mr. Watson entered, smiling as he saw Cain sitting in class. Class continues for the rest of the day as normal. Once class ends Dex, Cain, and Mr. Watson talk a little after class.

"I'm glad to see you're back, Cain. How're you feeling?" Mr. Watson asked.

"I'm good. Actually, better than ever," Cain responded, still not entirely sure of himself.

Dex, still hyped from earlier, couldn't help but chime in. "Yeah, with some new abilities too!"

"Dex!" Cain hissed, giving him a warning glance.

Cain quickly tried to explain himself. "Yeah, I'm eating a lot more and feel stronger, but it's weird."

"Well, I'm glad you're better," Mr. Watson said. "Let me know if you need anything, Cain. That goes for you too, Dex."

Dex grabbed Cain and pulled him to the other side of the room, whispering. "Cain, I really think we need to tell an adult about all this. And I vote for Mr. Watson. He's a doctor, maybe he knows something about this Dr. Vial guy."

Cain looked at him, unsure. "I don't know... I just feel like we can't keep this to ourselves anymore. Breezy and Tony know now, and things are getting out of hand."

They walked back over to Mr. Watson, both of them hesitant to speak up. Clark looked up at them, his eyebrow up in concern.

"You guys okay?" he asked.

Cain took a deep breath. *"Hey, Mr. Watson, what if I told you someone could... I don't know, control or throw lightning?"*

Mr. Watson chuckled. *"I'd say you've been watching too much TV."*

Cain stayed silent for a moment, before suddenly thrusting his hand out. A bolt of lightning shot from his palm, hitting the wall with a loud crack.

He turned to Dex. *"I think I'm getting used to this."*

Mr. Watson's face went pale. He sat back in his chair, stunned by what he had just witnessed.

Chapter 22

Sickled Shock

Cain's sudden display of power left everyone in silence. Clark blinked, trying to shake the image of the lightning strike from his mind. For a moment, he wondered if he'd imagined it, but the scorch mark on the wall told a different story. Dex, being Dex, looked at the scorched wall.

"Sooo, how are we going to hide that?" he asked, pointing at the wall.

Clark finally found his words. *"Cain, do you have…"*

Dex stopped him mid-sentence. "*Powers!? Yeah, isn't that sweet!*" Dex grinned, his excitement noticeable.

"*Yeah. I'm honestly not sure what it is or how to use them properly. That was only my third time using it. The first two were accidents,*" Cain explained.

Clark got up and closed the door.

"*Before you yell at us, sorry about your wall. We didn't know who to tell, so here we are.*"

Clark sat back down. "*No, no, it's okay. Forget the wall. You said this was the third time? If you don't mind me asking, when and where did this happen, and who saw you?*"

"*No one has really seen it, like you and Dex just now, but I accidentally used it on Breezy—well, Brixton—and Tony. The other time was at the hospital, not long after I woke up from the lab incident. I accidentally used it on some doctor who wasn't really a doctor, I don't think.*"

Clark sat up straighter. "*Cain, please don't tell me it was... Dr. Vial.*"

Cain looked at Dex, and Dex looked back at Cain.

"*Oh! This is serious!*" Clark said, his concern growing. "*No more talking about this here. Would you two be open to meeting at my house after school today?*"

Dex shrugged, and Cain agreed to meet after school. The two walked out of the classroom.

"Hey, Cain, that was crazy back there. Do you know how to control it now?" Dex asked.

"Honestly, no. But I hope I can start controlling it. I'm more worried about this Dr. Vial guy. Mr. Watson seemed pretty afraid—or at least worried—when he found out," Cain replied.

"Yeah, he was stuck on that more than you sending a bolt of lightning into his wall..." Dex paused, his thoughts taking a turn. "Wait, if this is really you becoming a hero, you need a name. Oh, I need a secret name too if I'm going to be your sidekick."

Cain laughed, hoping Dex would let it go.

"No, seriously. I'll come up with something. Just you wait, Cain. I got this." The two continued on with their day and went on to the rest of their classes.

Hours later, after class, Cain called his parents to tell them he was staying after school to make up some work with Dex and Mr. Watson. Dex didn't call his parents, as he was always at Cain's house after school anyway. Cain and Dex were now back in Mr. Watson's class, ready to ride with him to his house. On the way there, Cain explained everything that had happened the night at the hospital. Mr.

Watson listened intently, taking in every detail and trying to figure out how to stop Dr. Vial.

He then told Dex what he knew about Dr. Vial. "Now, I need you two to understand. Right now, I'm no longer your teacher. This is a serious matter outside of school. Dr. Vial has been known to do some inhumane things. He has a basement lab in his garage with vials of blood from patients over the years. I personally don't know what he does with them, but I've seen his lab in person. It's something out of the ordinary for sure. If he gets a hold of your powers, Cain, who knows what could happen."

They pulled up to Mr. Watson's house and went inside. Clark pulled out a notebook and began writing a summary of everything Cain had told him in the car. Dex, always ready to break the tension, noticed that Clark had mentioned he wasn't their teacher anymore.

"Hey, teach, I know you said outside of school you're not our teacher, but wouldn't it be cool if we had names like actual heroes?"

Cain shook his head, trying not to laugh at how ridiculous Dex sounded. Dex looked at Cain and threw his hands up.

"What? I'm just saying."

Clark added, *"Honestly, you have a point, and it wouldn't be a bad idea. Dr. Vial's name isn't Dr. Vial, believe it or not."*

Dex looked at Cain. *"See? I told you..."*

Ring! Ring! Ring!

Dex was cut off by the high-pitched ringing of Clark's phone.

"Hello?" Clark answered, listening intently.

"Uhm, yes, this is Clark Watson. Who is this?" he asked.

The silence in the room was thick as Clark listened to whoever was on the other end of the phone. Cain and Dex exchanged worried glances, concerned that it might be Dr. Vial.

"What if Mr. Watson is setting us up?" Cain whispered.

"Relax, teach wouldn't do that. He cares too much about us. You should've seen him at the hospital after school that day you got shocked," Dex reassured him.

"Uh, yeah. Sure, you can come by here, that's fine," Clark said into the phone.

Click! The phone hung up.

"So, we're not the only ones looking for Dr. Vial it seems. Strangely enough, that was a nurse from the hospital. She went by the school just now, but since I wasn't there, she got my number from someone. She's claiming she heard a story about

me and Dr. Vial and wants to figure out a way to take him down."

Cain was still on edge, second-guessing the situation, while Dex didn't see anything wrong and continued with the talk about being a superhero team and coming up with names.

"So, teach, about these names. With Cain having these powers and us working as his partners, we can't just go as Cain, Dex, and Mr. Watson. We must be secretive, right?"

Mr. Watson looked at Cain. "This kid doesn't give up on things when he has his mind set on something, does he, Cain?"

Cain shook his head.

"I mean, yeah, Dex, you're right, but we have to worry about Dr. Vial right now," Clark said, noticing Dex's disappointed expression.

"Hey, Mr. Watson," Cain said, nodding at him to look at Dex. "Let's hear him out, then we can move on, maybe."

"Okay, Dex. What are you thinking with these names?"

Dex stood up, smiling, and began shooting off names. "I thought about for you, Mr. Watson, either 'Teach' still, 'Mr. Cool,' 'Doctor CW,' and then for me, I was thinking 'Chip,' 'Ctrl,' or 'DexByte' since I'm pretty good with technology, you know. And for Cain... ah man, like 'Thunderous Hero,'

'Thunder Blood.' I could go on for a while with Cain's names."

Cain and Mr. Watson exchanged a glance, holding back laughs at how terrible the names sounded as Dex continued.

"Oh, I got it! This is a good one—hear me out— what about 'Thunderous Blood! The Hero with Sickle Cell!'"

Knock! Knock! Knock!

Dex sat down, now nervous, as Cain stood up. Mr. Watson looked toward the door. Dex noticed Cain's tense posture, his eyes once again sparking with energy. Mr. Watson opened the door.

"Hey, Mr. Watson, right? My name is Elaine, I called you not too long ago."

"Oh, yes, come in." Mr. Watson stepped aside, checking to make sure she wasn't being followed.

Elaine entered the house, and Cain stood still, unsure what to expect. Dex sat quietly, but Elaine didn't notice Cain's eyes from where she stood.

Dex turned to Cain. "Hey, bro, relax. She seems pretty normal."

Cain sat back down, and the static shock in his pupils disappeared. Mr. Watson closed and locked the door behind them, then returned to the living room.

"Dex, Cain, this is Elaine. Elaine, these are my students, just here talking about what our next science class will be about."

"Hello, ma'am, nice to meet you," both Cain and Dex said.

Elaine stood still for a moment, her gaze lingering on Cain. She had officially run into the boy she had been told about—*Patient Sickled Shock*. Clark, now slightly confused, hoped he had gotten her name right when introducing everyone.

"Wait, it is Elaine, right?" he asked.

Elaine snapped out of her thoughts, realizing Clark was talking. "*I'm sorry, yes, my name is Elaine. Hello, nice to meet you two as well. I'm sorry, I was just thinking about something and zoned out.*"

"So, what were you saying on the phone?" Clark asked.

Elaine seemed lost in thought again, but finally answered, "*Uhh, yeah.*" She whispered, "*Can we talk in front of them?*"

Clark looked at Dex and Cain. "Yeah, truthfully, I think we all have the same problem somehow. Honestly, I'm not sure how this happened."

Elaine, now certain that this was *Patient Sickled Shock*, spoke up. "*So, you guys weren't talking about school? This is about Dr. Vial as well?*" she asked.

Cain stood up, still suspicious, while Dex continued to speak. "You know Dr. Vial?"

Elaine nodded. "I know what he does and how he goes after people. I also think I know a little about someone in this room as well, but I'm not 100% certain just yet."

Cain's eyes began to spark again. Elaine noticed and instantly questioned him. "So... so... so... you're Baby Cain? Well, not so 'baby' anymore, but you're Cain."

Dex, noticing the sparks, intervened. "Heyyy Cain, bro, let's hear her out, you know? Sit down and talk about everything."

Cain calmed down, and they all sat to talk, sharing everything they knew. Elaine even told them about 16 years ago and all about Van.

"So, if Van was so interested in my life and helping me, making sure I'm living well, why isn't she here now to stop Dr. Vial with you? Did something happen to her?" Cain asked.

"She would've been here, but she's sick. She has cancer and is just having a bad day today," Elaine explained.

Dex, breaking the tension as usual, added, "Dang, does this mean I have to come up with two new names now for you and Miss Van?"

Clark shook his head as Cain looked down. "He wants to come up with alias names so bad. I'll just start you off, Dex. I'll go by Professor Dark." Clark states.

Dex grinned. "That's a good one. Why didn't I think of that? Dang, well, I'll go by DexByte then."

Cain looked at Dex. "Bro, your name is Dex! How is your so-called secret name going to be DexByte?"

"You're right. Just call me Byte then, like gigabyte or something, you know. What about you, though, Cain?"

"I'm not sure yet. Maybe..." Cain trailed off, thinking.

The silence was broken by the loud ringing of a phone on speaker.

Click!

"*Hello?*" came a soft, raspy voice from Elaine's phone.

"*Van! Finish this sentence. Patient... what?*"

Van calmly and slightly with a confused soft voice says back. "Sickled Shock?"

Cain, Dex, and Clark stared at Elaine as she smirked listening to the response from Van.

Chapter 23

The Ultimate Plan

Van's raspy voice slipped through the phone. The words "Sickled Shock" echoed in Cain's mind long after Van's voice had faded, leaving him paralyzed with questions. Who was Van really, and what did she know about him that he didn't?

Elaine went on to inform Van of the current situation. She told Van that she was sitting with Cain and that they planned to take Dr. Vial and his operations down.

Elaine muted the phone and looked over at Cain. *"Would you like to talk to Van? She's really been worried about you for 16 years now."*

Cain shrugged, still not knowing who Van was or why she had been looking for him. *"Sure, I don't mind."*

Elaine unmuted the phone and handed it to Cain. *"Hello, Miss Van?"*

Van went quiet, now having officially heard the voice of Cain—"Patient Sickled Shock" Lorane. *"Hi, is this baby Cain?"*

Cain looked at Elaine, confused, mouthing baby Cain? Elaine nodded, confirming it. *"Yes, ma'am. I believe so."*

Cain could hear sniffles from the other end of the phone as Van was overwhelmed with emotion and joy upon hearing Cain's voice. She let out some tears. Van quickly composed herself and continued, telling Cain how everything started and how she knew him. The conversation lasted for about 20 minutes, going back and forth.

Van finished, *"I'm sorry, Cain. I know I couldn't have changed that night when you got shocked, but I'm sorry for treating you like an experiment alongside Sam without knowing his intent. Instead, I should've treated you like the amazing human you've turned out to be. You sound like a lovely young man, and I'm so happy to hear your voice for the first time. I wish I could've seen you today, but hearing the voice of a warrior is good enough. Glad you're well. Keep fighting sickle cell and* conquer the world with everyone by your side. Tell Elaine I said thank you and I love her, as it did all come full circle. Fight on, Cain!"

Cain took it all in before responding, "No need for you to be sorry, Miss Van. I appreciate everything. I'll do as you say and continue my fight with sickle cell and anything else that comes my way, starting with Dr. Vial. Thank you again, Miss Van, and I'll tell Elaine."

It was silent for a moment before Van, obviously crying again, spoke. "Lightning in your veins, Thunder in your soul! You got this, Sickled Shock."

Click! The phone hung up, and a small tear slid down Cain's face.

He inhaled deeply, wiped his face, and let out a huge exhale. "That is one wonderful and powerful lady." Cain handed the phone back to Elaine. "She told me to tell you, Elaine, that she said thank you and she loves you."

"Aww, I love her too!"

"She also said to tell you it all ended up coming full circle after all. Not sure what that means exactly."

Elaine sat in disbelief. "Oh wow. She warned me 16 years ago not to be surprised if all of this doesn't come back full circle. And look at us now."

"Sooo, Sickled Shock! You ready to stop this Dr. Vial guy?" Dex said.

Mr. Watson nudged Dex. "You really know how to ruin a moment or break the tension within the room, don't you, Dex?" This made everyone in the room laugh.

Cain shook his head. "He really does, but he's right, despite the bad timing. So how should we go about this? Any plans, Professor Dark?"

As everyone started going by their new alias names, they sat around, trying to come up with a plan to take down Dr. Vial. As the plans were slowly tossed around, no one seemed to know how to approach the situation. Byte (Dex) then came up with an idea that no one else had mentioned.

"Why don't we just call the police?"

Sickled Shock (Cain), Professor Dark (Clark Watson), and Elaine all looked at Byte.

"And say what exactly? This guy has stolen blood samples from the blood bank and is running an experiment in his house. Then they send out an officer to search an empty house? I don't think it's that easy, Byte," said Sickled Shock.

Professor Dark spoke up. "Yeah, he has a secret lair in his house hidden behind a keypad. Without that code, it's just a regular house."

Elaine, still in the shadows, hadn't been given a name yet, but she came up with an initial plan that might work. "*Sickled Shock, if you can, maybe you cut the power to the house, causing Dr. Vial to walk outside to check the power box. Once he's outside, Byte can sneak in from the back and through the house to unlock the front door, letting Professor Dark in. Once everyone's in, Sickled Shock powers the house back up.*"

Elaine was cut off. "*How do we get into the lair without the code?*" Professor Dark asked.

Byte and Sickled Shock exchanged a look. "*This is where Byte comes in. He should be able to make a device that can not only read and input the keycode but hack the keypad to open the door. Do you know where the pad is in the house, Professor?*"

"*Yeah, I do, actually.*"

Elaine continued, "*Great. Once Byte's in the house and unlocks the front door for Dark, we'll need a way to distract Dr. Vial while Byte and Dark reach the secret lair.*"

"*Wait, what do we do once we're in the lair?*" Byte asked.

Sickled Shock stood up, and his pupils began to spark with electricity. "*I'll handle the distraction and the lair!*" He threw his arm up, sending a bolt of lightning into Professor Dark's bedroom door.

"*You've got to be kidding me! My door now too?*" Professor Dark stood up, seeming a little mad and aggravated. "*You have to control that better, man!*"

Byte looked at the door, back at Sickled Shock, and then at Elaine. "*Wait, you need a name now!*" He said, simply ignoring the state of the door or what Sickled Shock had just done.

"*He's good at breaking tension,*" Elaine said. "*But no, I don't need one. I'm just a pharmacist doing the best for my friend. Not sure I'll be around for any more 'hero' tasks after this. Thanks for the thought though.*"

"*Sorry about your door, Professor. I'll fix it, but for now, Byte, you've got some work to do on that device.*"

With some sort of plan now in place, everyone got to work. Byte began building and preparing the device for the keypad, while Professor Dark tried to draw the layout of Dr. Vial's house so they wouldn't be going in blind. Sickled Shock spent hours practicing his abilities. Over time, he gained better control, eventually being able to send electrical charges out of his body, forming sparks and glowing light around him, and even holding a ball of lightning/electricity in his hand. While working, Byte caught Cain practicing.

"*Hey, you're really learning your powers pretty quickly. That's sick seeing the lightning in your hand like that.*"

The planning continued until sunset. Byte finally finished the device, and Sickled Shock had gained pretty good control over his powers after hours of training.

"So, what do you guys say?" asked Professor Dark. "Ready to head over to Dr. Vial's house and bring his whole operation to an end once and for all?"

Everyone looked around the room and collectively answered, "Let's do this!"

Chapter 24

Full Circle

With Elaine not officially being part of the team, she doesn't join them in going to Dr. Vials house. She would rather help from the shadows, assisting with plans or using her nursing and pharmacy skills for future endeavors. For now, she is focused on stopping Dr. Vial's mission from a far. Elaine could eventually be part of the team, but for now, she wants what's best for Van and Sickled Shock.

"Hey, fellas, I think my job here is done. I'll keep in contact with you. Dark, please let me know *how things go and stay safe out there. I'll be with Van to check on her, so call me ASAP."* Elaine leaves Professor Dark's house and heads to see Van.

"This is going to be fun. I'm so ready; it feels like I'm in a movie or something," Byte says, full of energy. *"Also, here, take these."* Byte hands Dark and Sickled Shock what appears to be a communication device or earbud that they can use while breaking in.

Dark looks at Byte with a concerned expression. *"Where or how did you make these, exactly, Byte?"*

Byte drops his head, afraid to answer. *"Let's just say I used a bunch of different items around your house to put together something quick. They could have been way better quality, but you lacked some things in this house for me to use."*

Byte slowly looks up at Professor Dark. *"Just to give a slight heads-up on some of the items I used... You may or may not need a new microwave to start. Just to name one item I used. I'm sorry."*

Professor Dark can't do anything but laugh. *"We'll get back to that another day. We need our own secret lair. You guys are destroying my house. Anyways, let's head out so we can get you two back home."*

Byte, Professor Dark, and Sickled Shock are now on their way to stop Dr. Vial from continuing his evil scientist habits. Pulling up to the house, Professor Dark parks about three houses down so Dr. Vial doesn't suspect anything. Once out of the car and approaching the house on foot, everyone places the homemade earbuds in their ears, testing if they work properly.

Hiding in the shadows of the streetlights across from the house, Dark whispers, *"Okay, fellas, that's the house over there."*

Sickled Shock throws his hood over his head, covering most of his eyes. *"Once you two see the power go out, stick to the plan. I'll handle the rest. I'll first figure out where his power box is, and Byte, you'll come in from the opposite side of the backyard."*

Sickled Shock walks away, leaving Dark and Byte waiting for the power to cut. Just over five minutes pass. A static sound from the earbud radios fills the air. *"Byte, come in from the left side of the backyard on my cue."*

Byte looks at Professor Dark. *"I'm actually scared now, Professor."* A sudden chill runs through Byte's body as the power in the house cuts, the kitchen and bedroom lights flickering off at the same time.

Professor Dark looks at the house. *"Well, looks like we have no choice now. Let's go!"*

The two run across the street, and Byte heads to the left side of the house while Dark waits at the front by a bush, awaiting the front door to be unlocked.

"In position," comes through the radio from Professor Dark, followed by silence.

The static sound comes over the radio again. *"Byte, I know you're probably nervous, but now is the chance to stand up and do something big. Think of this like we're fighting Breezy and Tony."* Sickled Shock says, followed by, *"Do it for me."*

There's a brief silence followed by Byte's nervous voice. *"In position."*

The timing is perfect. A flashlight comes on, shining from the back door. As planned, Dr. Vial heads to the electrical box. Byte notices and realizes this is his chance to move. He makes a run for the back door. Once inside, he takes a quick breath, feeling tired and nervous.

Dr. Vial stands at the electrical box, trying to fix it and noticing a distinct static coming from the box. Sickled Shock, now standing behind him, makes his move, but Dr. Vial speaks first, not even turning around.

"Well, well, well. Looks like you came to find me instead of me finding you first."

This throws Sickled Shock's plan off. Now, he must rethink the situation.

"*I should have known something was up when the power cut, without any storm or anything. So, what's your plan now that you've caught me off guard?*"

Sickled Shock shoots a bolt of lightning past Dr. Vial's head, hitting the power box in front of him and turning the power back on.

With the power back on, Byte looks up at the lights as they turn back on. He gets off the floor and sprints to the front door, letting Professor Dark in.

"*Let's go! We may be running out of time.*" Dark walks over and removes a picture frame from the wall, revealing the keypad. Byte looks up at Professor Dark and takes the device out of his backpack.

"*I really hope this works.*" Byte places the device on the keypad, realizing it's not getting enough power to operate. "*We're going to need more power to start this up, Professor! What do we do now?*" Byte says with panic in his voice.

Outside, with Dr. Vial and Sickled Shock.

"*My friends are in your house right now, shutting your little operation down as we speak!*" Sickled Shock says.

Dr. Vial turns around to see Sickled Shock standing behind him, hood covering most of his eyes. He glances over at his back door, which was obviously left open by Byte. The sound of the radio in Sickled Shock's ear crackles. *"Hey, we need extra power to get in fully."*

Sickled Shock shoots a bolt of lightning at Dr. Vial's feet, knocking him to the ground. He sprints to the back door, making it into the threshold. He charges up energy and sends it to the device, knocking Byte and Professor Dark away from the door and onto the ground, as well as causing Sickled Shock to faint at the back door.

The door to the lair opens. Byte gets up and cheers. *"We did it! It's opening!"* Professor Dark stands up and sees Dr. Vial standing over a fainted Sickled Shock. Dark proceeds to break rule number one.

He uses a name and breaks the code. *"Sam! Just stop. It's over. Give it all up. That's a kid! Do you have no respect?"*

Dr. Vial pulls out a needle just as his front door gets kicked in.

"FREEZE! Everyone put your hands up!"

As everyone in the house raises their hands, multiple cops walk in with guns drawn, and Elaine follows in shortly after the last officer. One of the cops approaches Dr. Vial with his gun still out.

"Sam Bloodworth, you're under arrest for illegal human experimentation, larceny, and other possible charges."

Byte drops his hands and runs over to Sickled Shock. Professor Dark looks at Elaine. "You came back! With help, I see."

Elaine looks at Dark. "There's no way I was going to let you three take down Sam Bloodworth without me being involved. I took some notes from Byte on calling the law, you know."

As the officer walks Dr. Vial out of the house, passing Elaine and Professor Dark, they stare at him. "I will be back, just you wait. You better be prepared. I'm not finished with this."

They now send Cain to the hospital and Sam to jail.

At the hospital, Cain slowly starts to wake up. Not in the ICU room as before, but surrounded by his father, mother, Dex, and Mr. Watson. As Cain blinks, he feels pain in his lower back, chest, and arms. It's his first major sickle cell crisis since the day of the lab.

Cain moves and groans. "Ahh, how long have I been here?"

Cain's mother gets up and walks to his bed. "A few hours now. Dex and Mr. Watson told us everything about how you weren't feeling good *while studying and then passed out during your makeup work. You should've called us, Cain."*

Cain looked over at Dex and Mr. Watson, realizing they came up with a lie to tell his parents instead of the truth about him having powers or what happened at the house of Sam Bloodworth.

"Yeah, mom, I know. I just wanted to get fully caught up on my schoolwork, that's all. I thought I could push through like always." Going along with the lie as he doesn't want everyone to know about his powers.

"I understand, baby. I'm just glad you're okay." She kisses Cain on the forehead and walks out of the room. Cain's dad fist bumps him. *"Love you, dude!"* and follows his mother out of the room, leaving Mr. Watson and Dex with Cain.

Dex jumps out of his chair. *"Dude, that was sick. I wish you could've seen it from our view. What did you do to Dr. Vial? He seemed pretty rattled once he walked in the back door. Bro, you're literally a superhero now."*

Mr. Watson gets up and walks over to Cain. *"How are you feeling, Cain?"*

Cain smirks at Dex and looks up at Mr. Watson. *"I'm good, just having a sickle cell crisis right now, apparently. But that's all. Don't really remember too much after I threw the charge at the device on the wall."*

"Well, it's good you're awake. I'm sure Dex will fill you in on everything that's happened. We were worried about you."

"Yeah, I'll be fine." Cain looks over at Dex. "I'm sure he will fill me in for sure. Did the plan work out in the end though?"

"It did, with the help of Elaine."

"Elaine? Oh yeah, sounds like I do need to be filled in about everything."

Dex picks up Cain's hand, observing it. "Hey, bro, you still think you have those powers?"

Elaine walks into the room, cutting off Cain's answer. Dex drops Cain's hand, and everyone focuses on Elaine as she walks in with obvious red eyes from crying.

Cain looks down at his hand as a tiny spark of light flickers, still showing he has some powers left. It's just a matter of getting better now. Elaine walks further into the room as everyone stares at her. Mr. Watson breaks the silence as Cain's hand still sparks.

"How is Van?" asks Mr. Watson.

Elaine smiles softly. "It all came full circle."

"I can't defeat Bryan"

\- Sickle Cell

Other titles by author Bryan Ballard; Sickled Life:

"Living the Sickled Life; A Sickle Cell Warrior's Story" - A book written and lived by a Sickle Cell Warrior. He tells the story of growing up with Sickle Cell, also how he gets through his life on a day to day managing his life. All while teaching the reader about Sickle Cell.

"Sickled Life, and Friends Activity Book (Volume 1)" - Activity book with coloring, and fun games all while learning about Sickle Cell Anemia. Fun for kids and adults of all ages. Dive into Sickle Cell with the help of the fun characters Sickled and Life.

Thanks again for the Love, and Support!

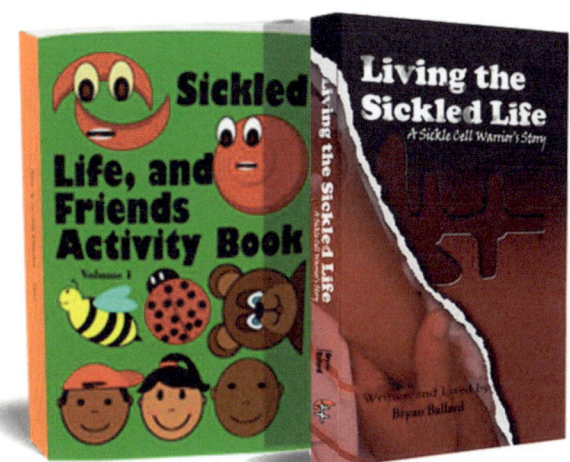

Available while supplies last

sickledlife.com

Made in the USA
Columbia, SC
01 March 2025

54521443R00109